D0853258

JOHNNY BOO FINDS A CLUE?

Hi!

JAMES KOCHALKA

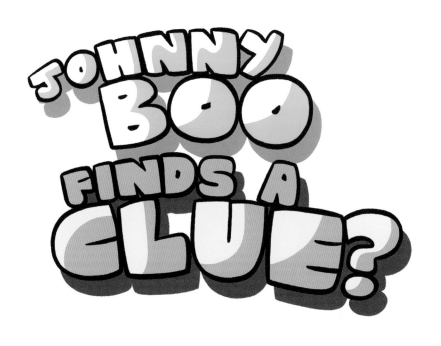

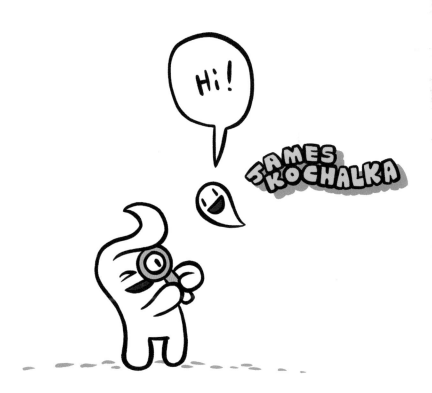

TOP SHELF PRODUCTIONS

A MAGNET FLY IN GLASS

Johnny Boo Finds a Clue? © 2020 James Kochalka.

Published by Top Shelf Productions, an imprint of IDW Publishing, a division of Idea and Design Works, LLC. Offices: Top Shelf Productions, c/o Idea & Design Works, LLC, 2765 Truxtun Road, San Diego, CA 92106. Top Shelf Productions®, the Top Shelf logo, Idea and Design Works®, and the IDW logo are registered trademarks of Idea and Design Works, LLC. All Rights Reserved. With the exception of small excerpts of artwork used for review purposes, none of the contents of this publication may be reprinted without the permission of IDW Publishing. IDW Publishing does not read or accept unsolicited submissions of ideas, stories, or artwork.

Editor-in-Chief: Chris Staros.

Edited by Leigh Walton.

Designed by Gilberto Lazcano & Tara McCrillis.

Visit our online catalog at www.topshelfcomix.com.

Printed in China.

ISBN 978-1-60309-476-4   23 22 21 20   4 3 2 1

CHAPTER ONE

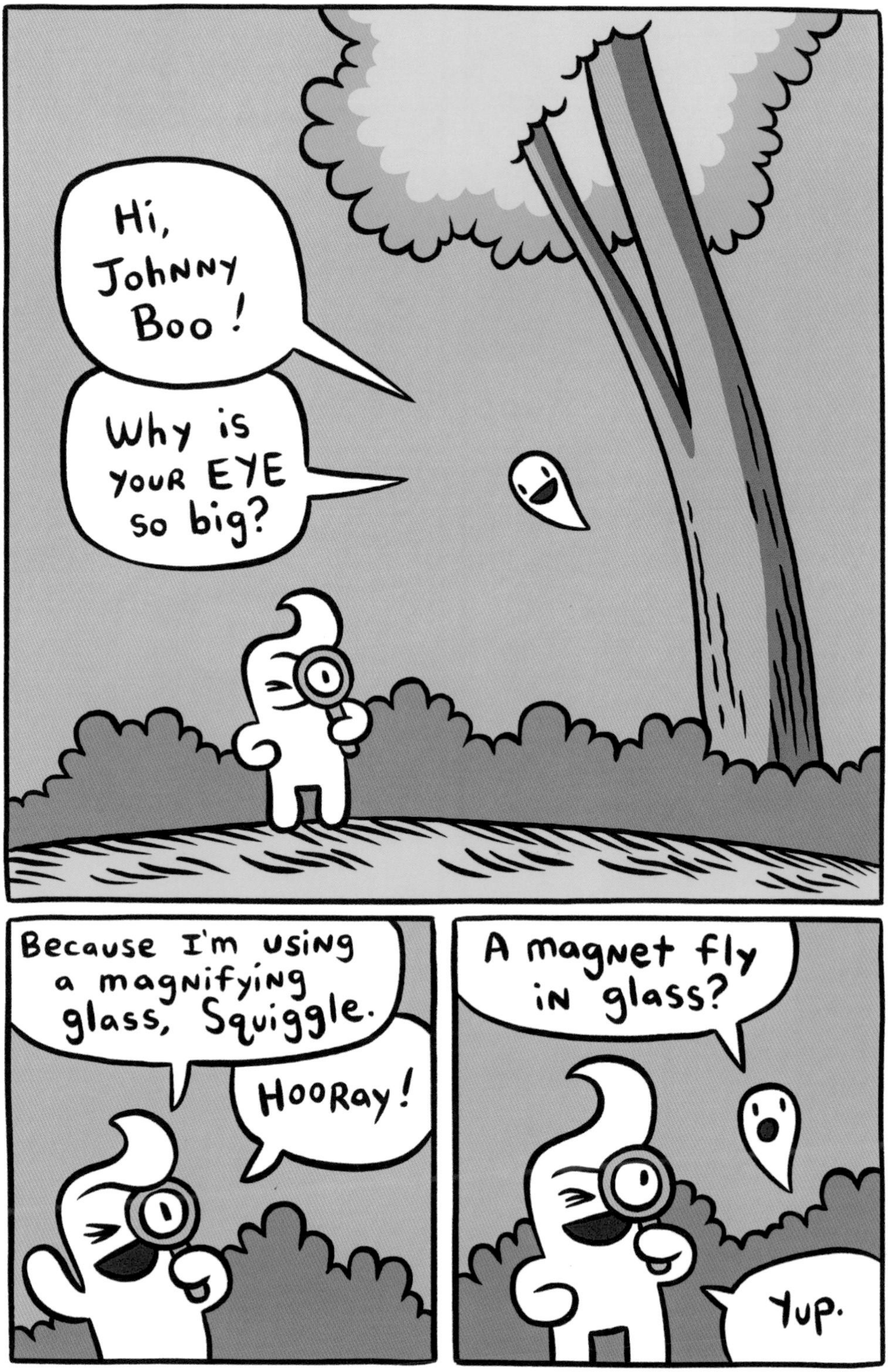
Hi, Johnny Boo!
Why is your EYE so big?
Because I'm using a magnifying glass, Squiggle.
HOORAY!
A magnet fly in glass?
Yup.

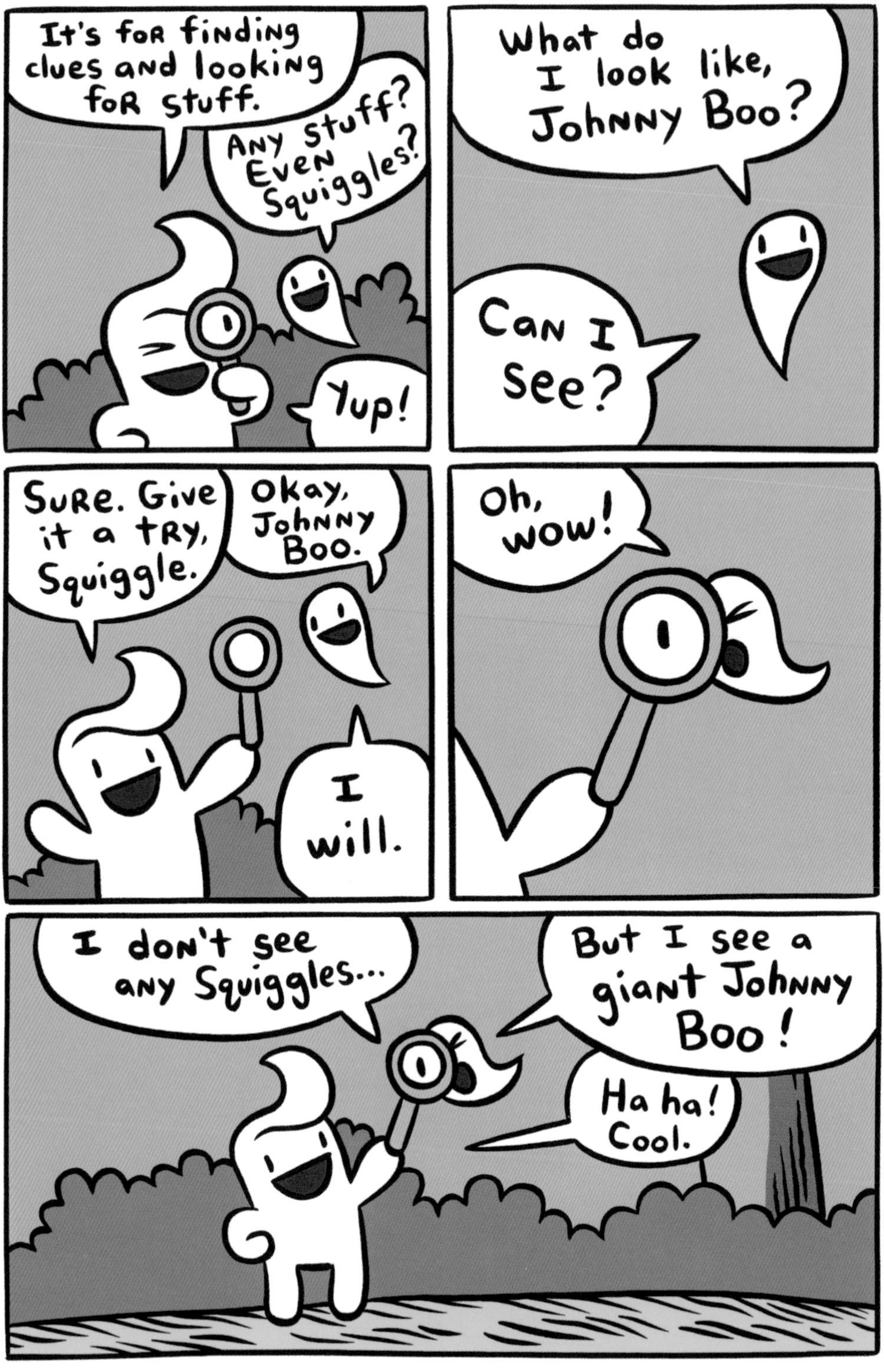
It's for finding clues and looking for stuff.
Any stuff? Even Squiggles?
Yup!
What do I look like, Johnny Boo?
Can I see?
Sure. Give it a try, Squiggle.
Okay, Johnny Boo.
I will.
Oh, wow!
I don't see any Squiggles...
But I see a giant Johnny Boo!
Ha ha! Cool.

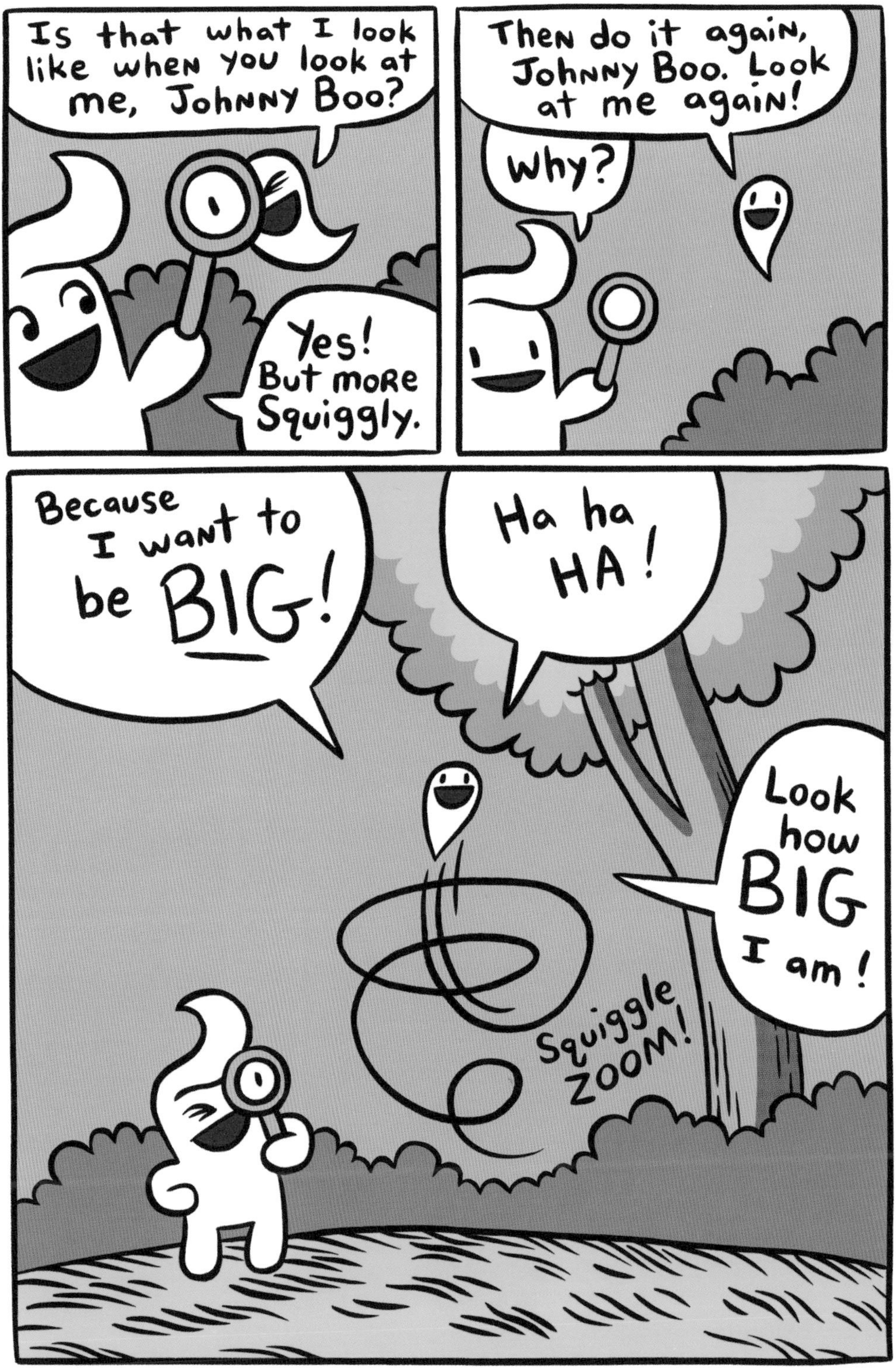
Is that what I look like when you look at me, Johnny Boo?
Yes! But more Squiggly.
Then do it again, Johnny Boo. Look at me again!
Why?
Because I want to be BIG!
Ha ha HA!
Look how BIG I am!
Squiggle ZOOM!

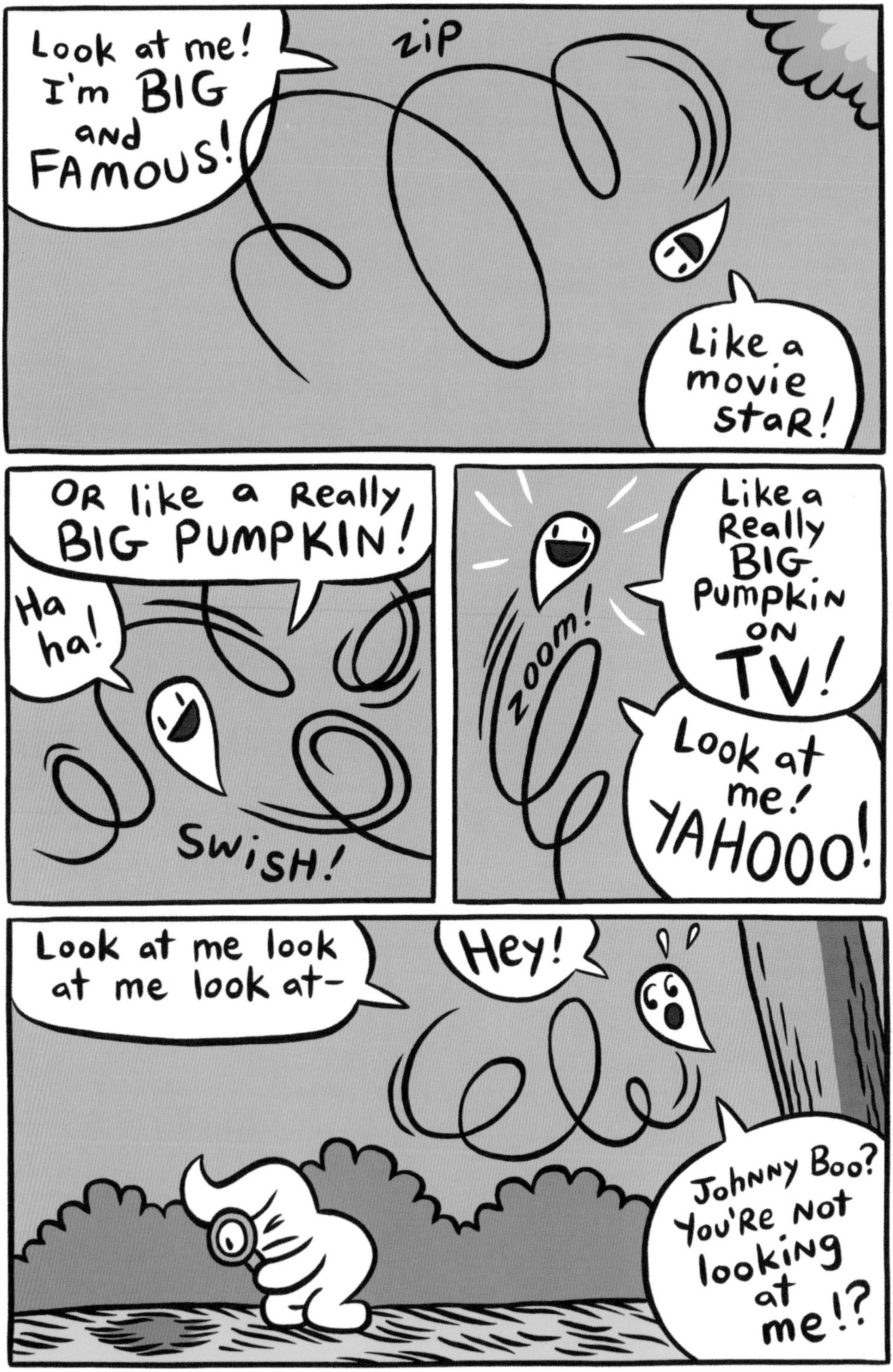
Look at me! I'm BIG and FAMOUS!
zip
Like a movie star!
OR like a Really BIG PUMPKIN!
Ha ha!
SWISH!
zoom!
Like a Really BIG Pumpkin ON TV!
Look at me! YAHOOO!
Look at me look at me look at-
Hey!
Johnny Boo? You're Not looking at me!?

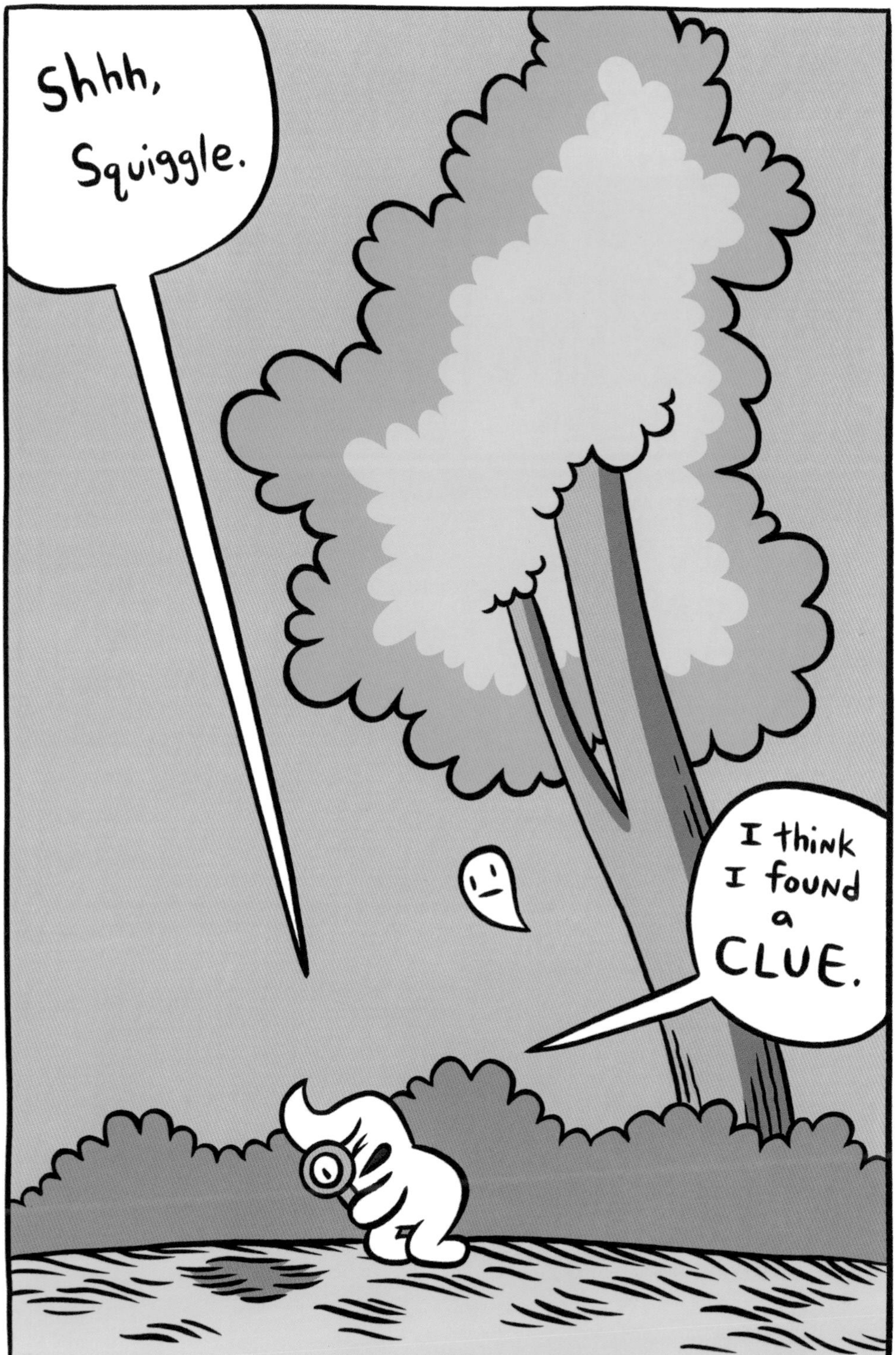
Shhh, Squiggle.
I think I found a CLUE.

CHAPTER TWO

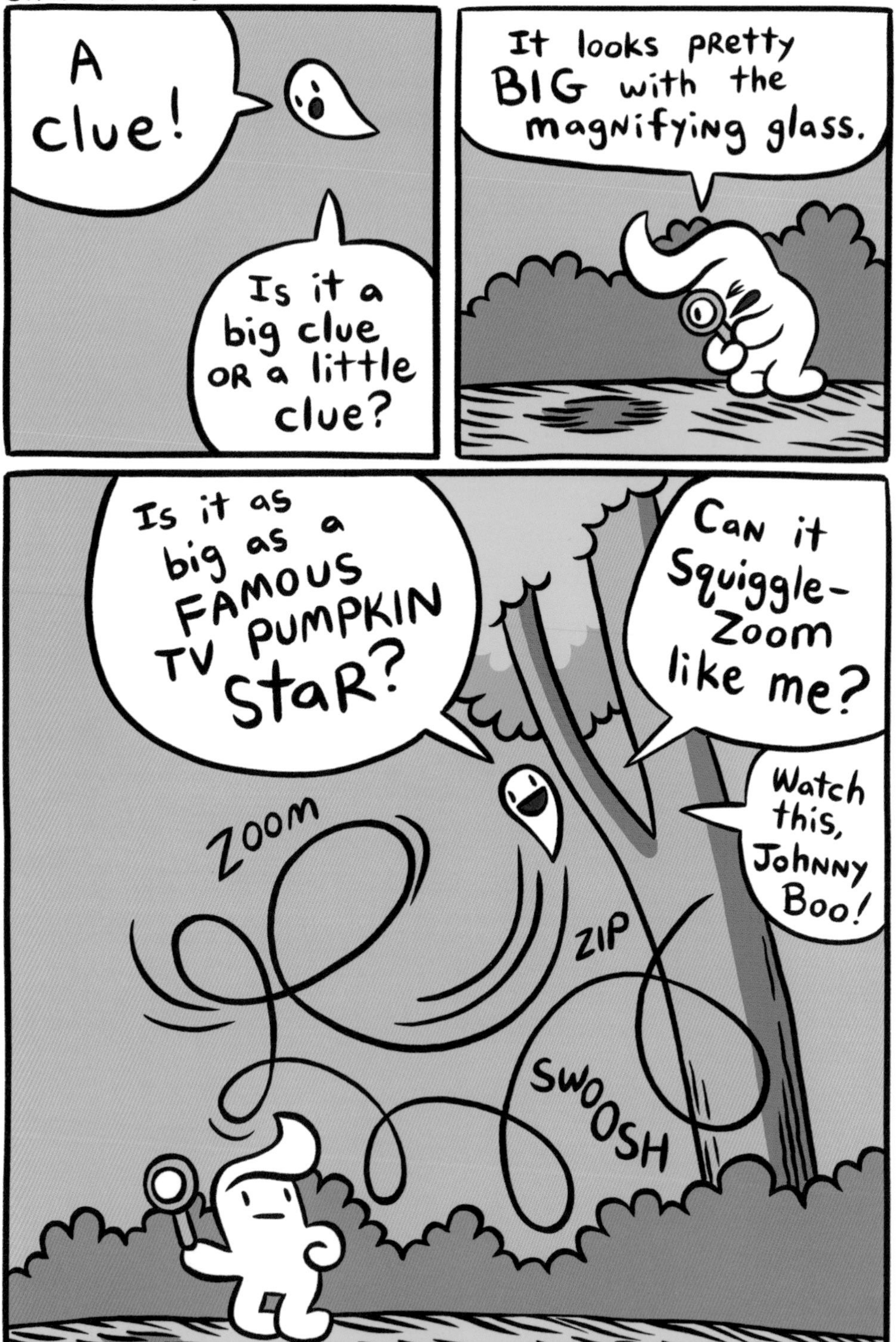
A clue!
Is it a big clue or a little clue?
It looks pretty BIG with the magnifying glass.
Is it as big as a FAMOUS PUMPKIN TV STAR?
Can it Squiggle-Zoom like me?
Watch this, Johnny Boo!
ZOOM
ZIP
SWOOSH

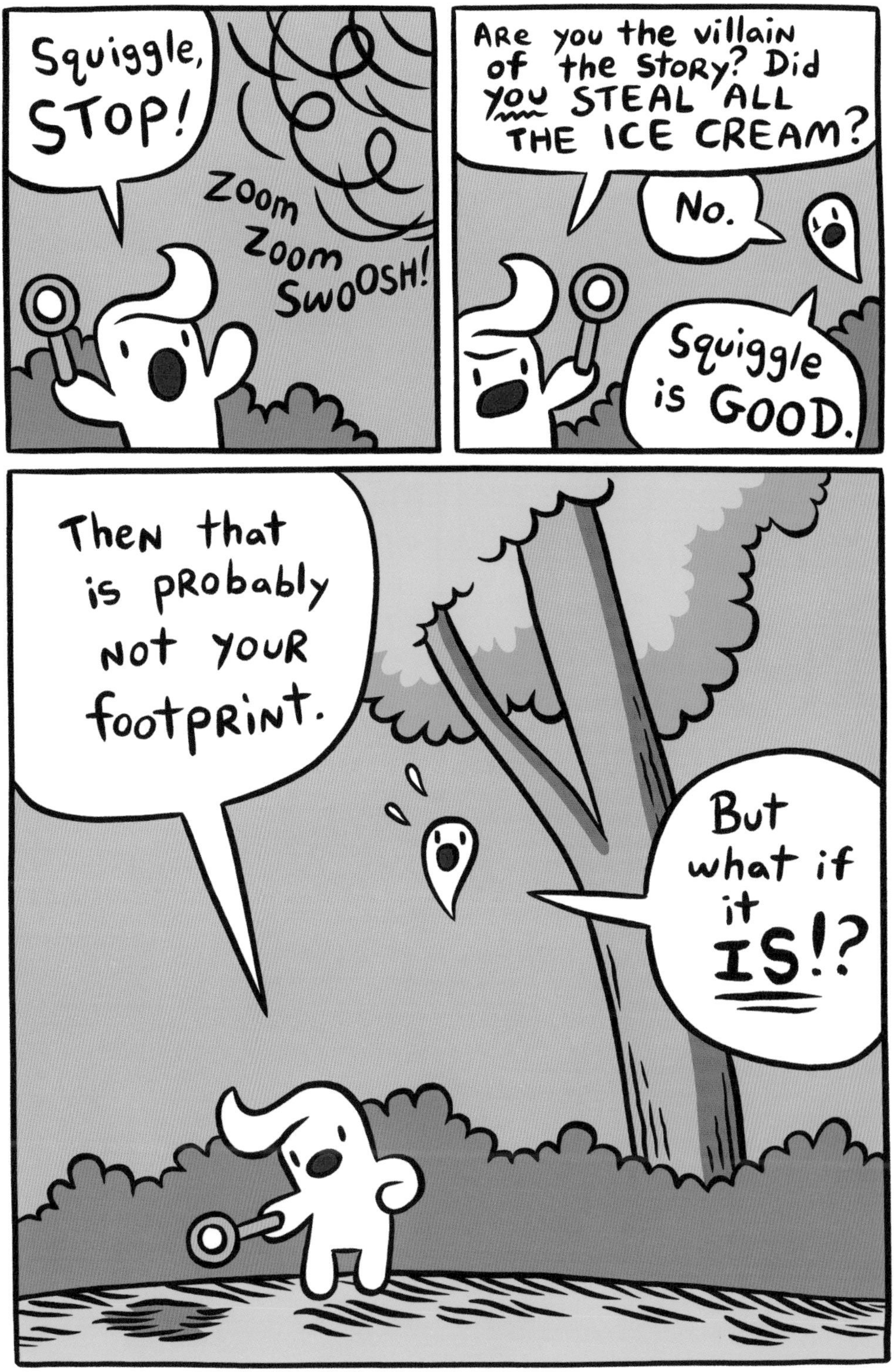

Squiggle, STOP!
Zoom Zoom SWOOSH!
Are you the villain of the story? Did YOU STEAL ALL THE ICE CREAM?
No.
Squiggle is GOOD.
Then that is probably not your footprint.
But what if it IS!?

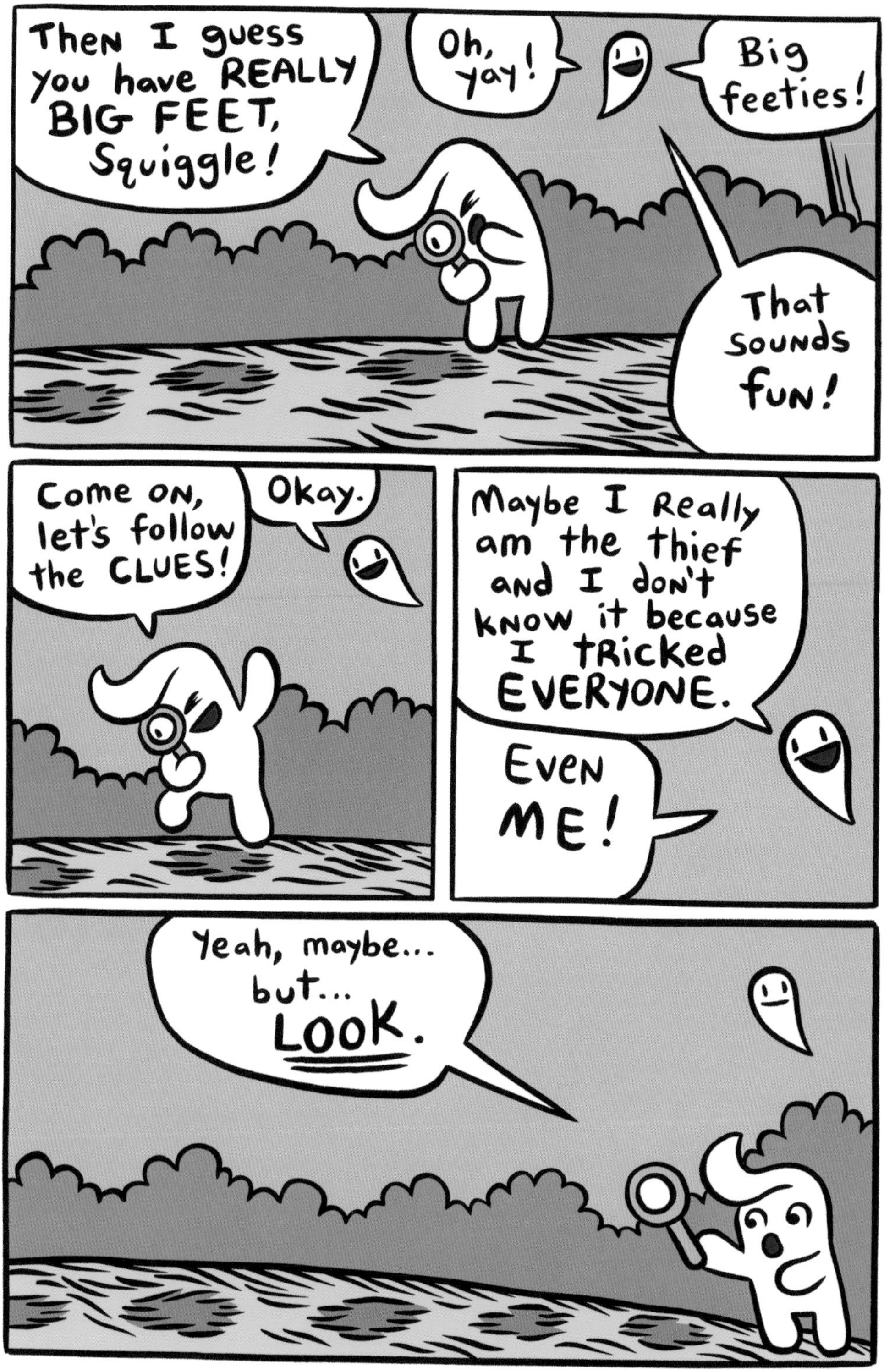
Then I guess you have REALLY BIG FEET, Squiggle!
Oh, yay!
Big feeties!
That sounds fun!
Come on, let's follow the CLUES!
Okay.
Maybe I really am the thief and I don't know it because I tricked EVERYONE.
Even ME!
Yeah, maybe... but... LOOK.

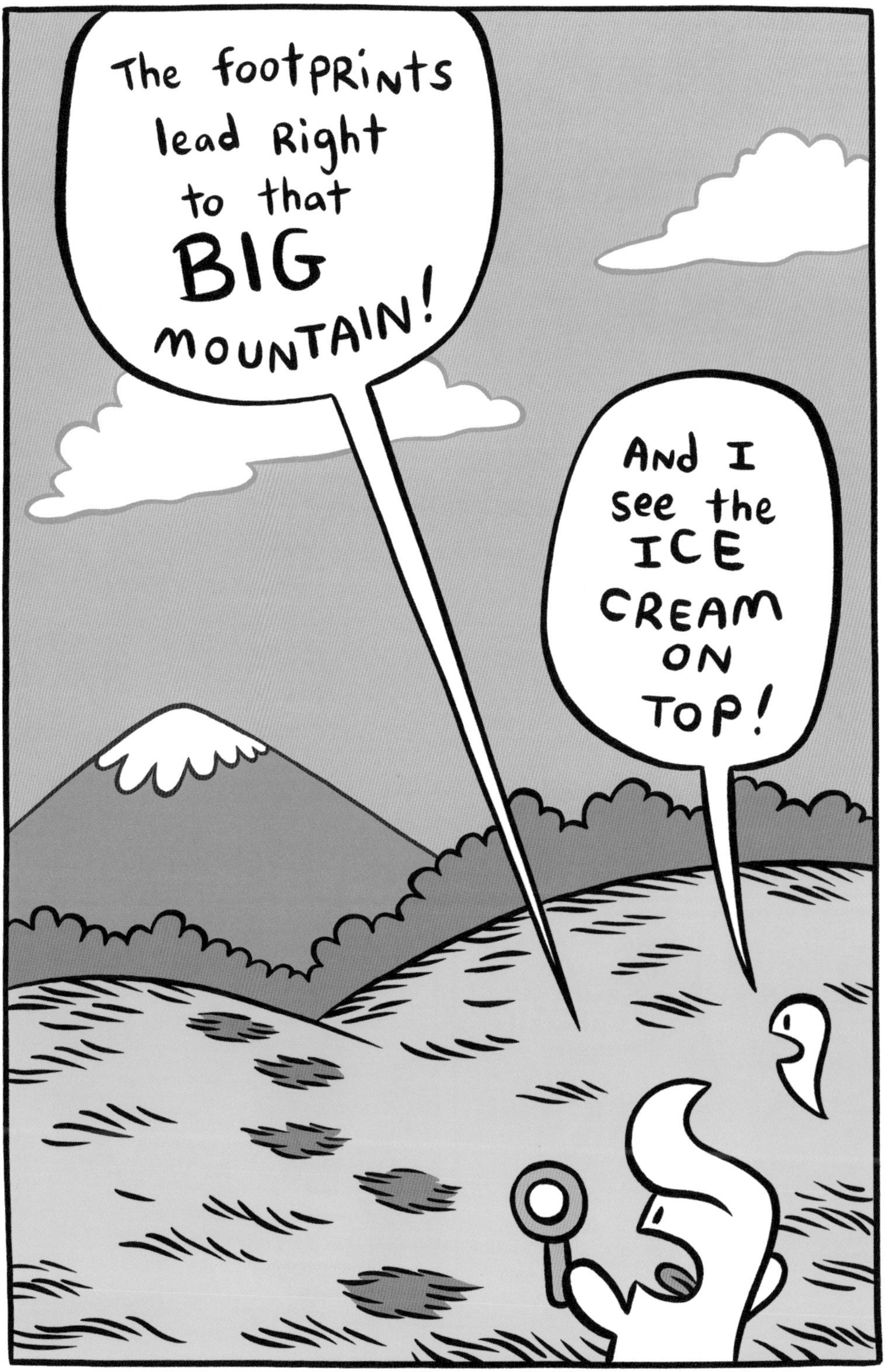
The footprints lead right to that BIG MOUNTAIN!
And I see the ICE CREAM ON TOP!

CHAPTER THREE

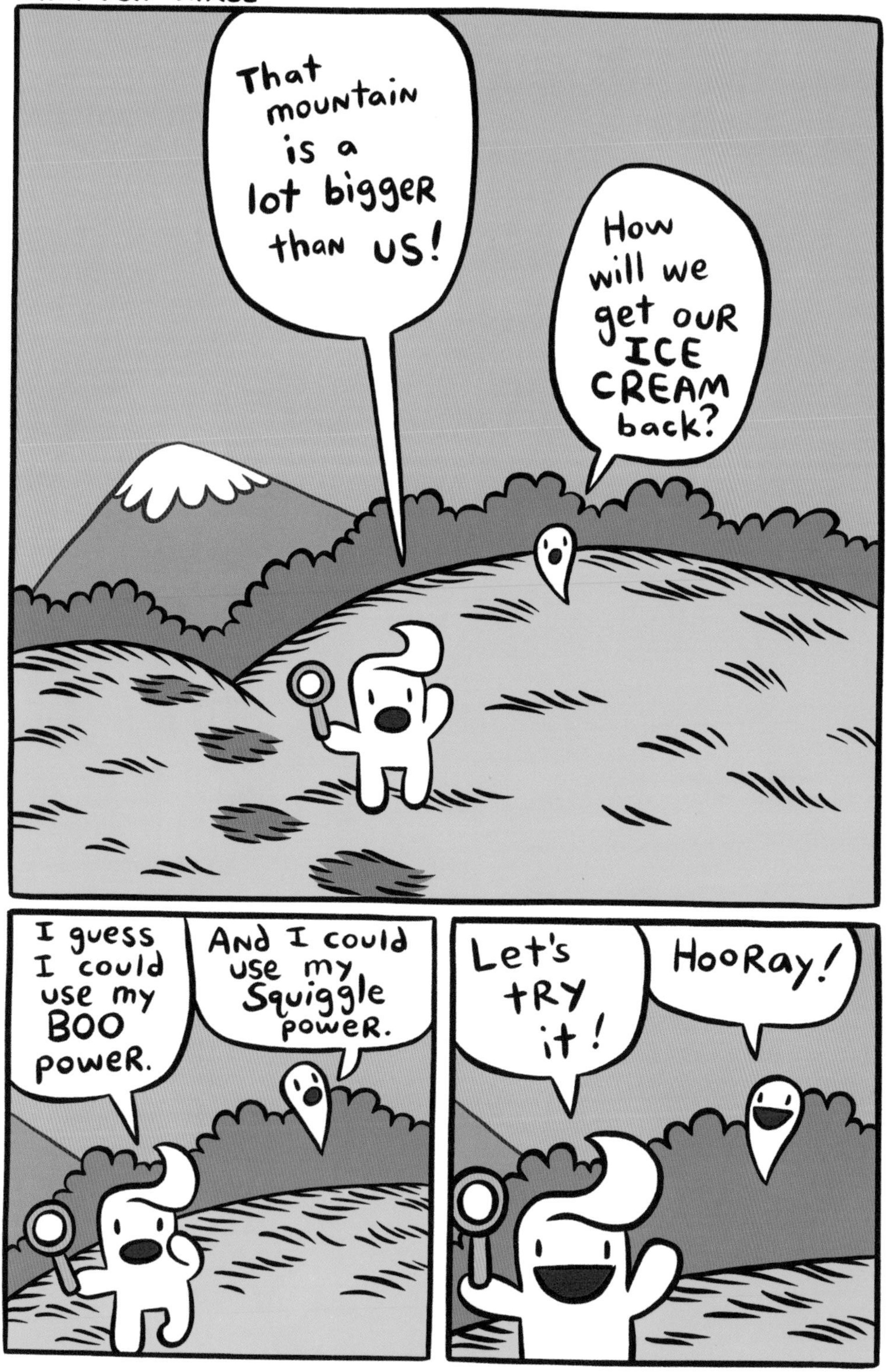
That mountain is a lot bigger than US!
How will we get our ICE CREAM back?
I guess I could use my BOO power.
And I could use my Squiggle power.
Let's try it!
Hooray!

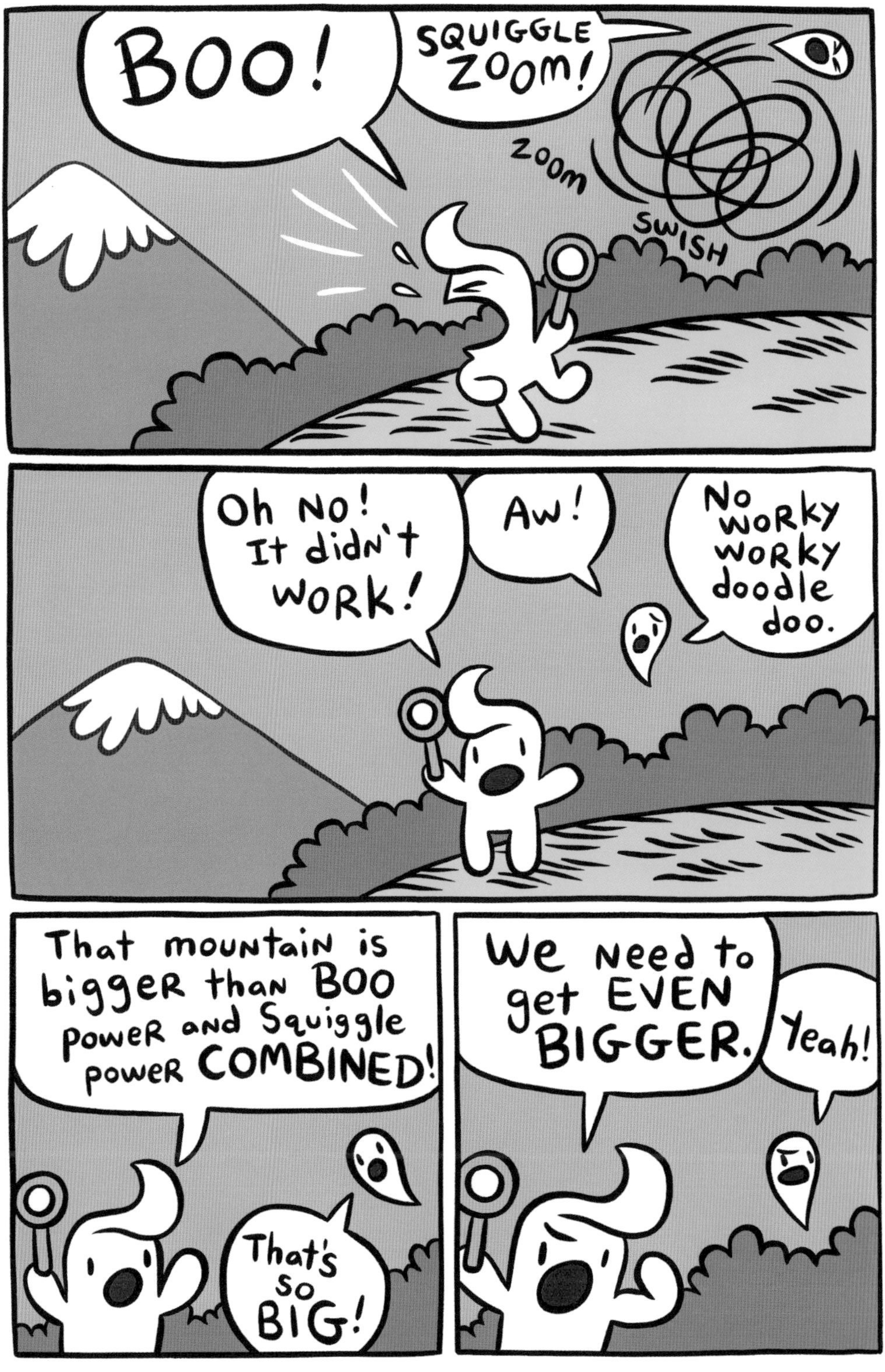
BOO!
SQUIGGLE ZOOM!
ZOOM
SWISH
Oh No! It didn't WORK!
Aw!
No worky worky doodle doo.
That mountain is bigger than BOO power and Squiggle power COMBINED!
That's so BIG!
We need to get EVEN BIGGER.
Yeah!

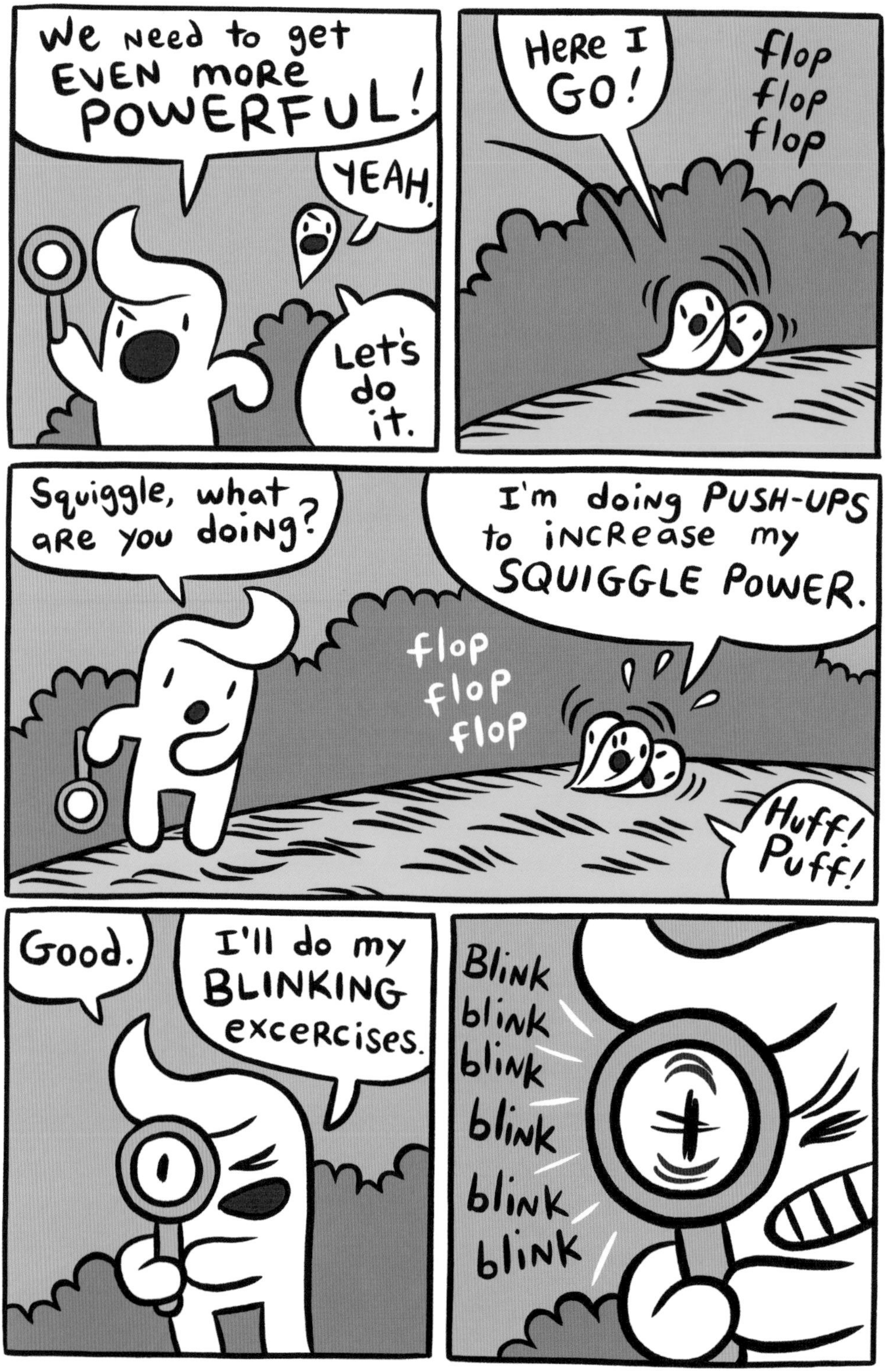
We need to get EVEN more POWERFUL!
YEAH.
Let's do it.
Here I GO!
flop flop flop
Squiggle, what are you doing?
I'm doing PUSH-UPS to increase my SQUIGGLE POWER.
flop flop flop
Huff! Puff!
Good.
I'll do my BLINKING excercises.
Blink blink blink blink blink blink

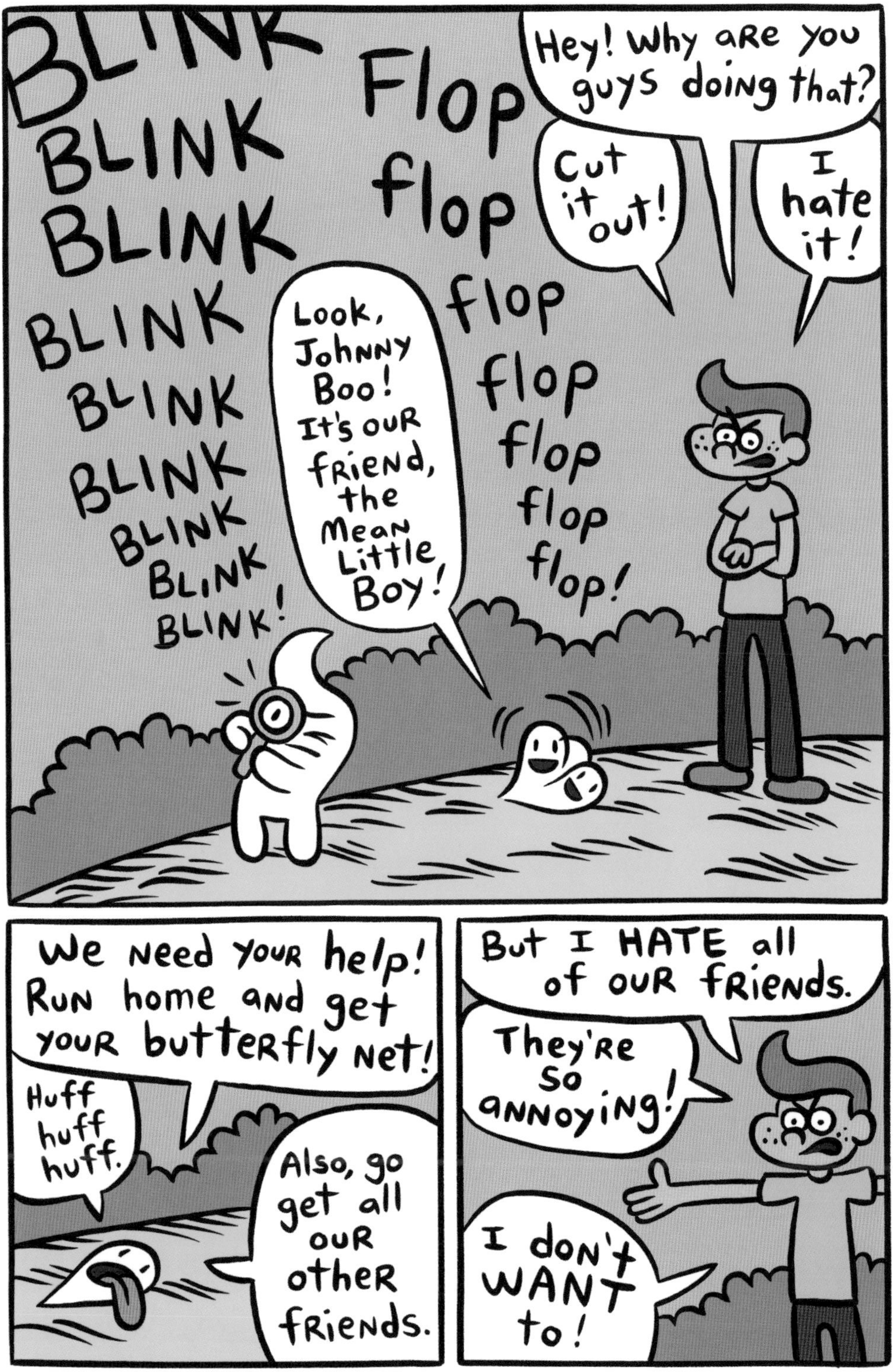
BLINK BLINK BLINK BLINK BLINK BLINK BLINK BLINK BLINK!
Flop flop flop flop flop flop flop!
Hey! Why are you guys doing that?
Cut it out!
I hate it!
Look, Johnny Boo! It's our friend, the Mean Little Boy!
We need your help! Run home and get your butterfly net!
Huff huff huff.
Also, go get all our other friends.
But I HATE all of our friends.
They're so annoying!
I don't WANT to!

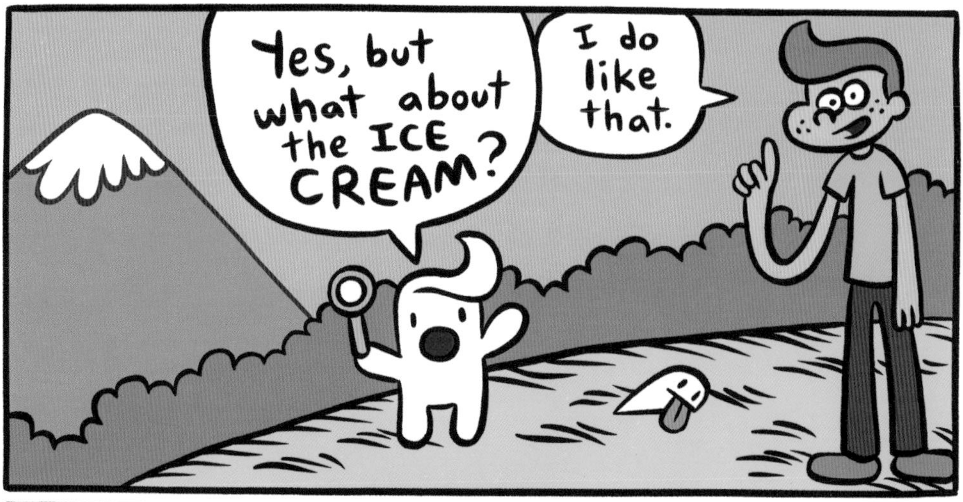
Yes, but what about the ICE CREAM?
I do like that.

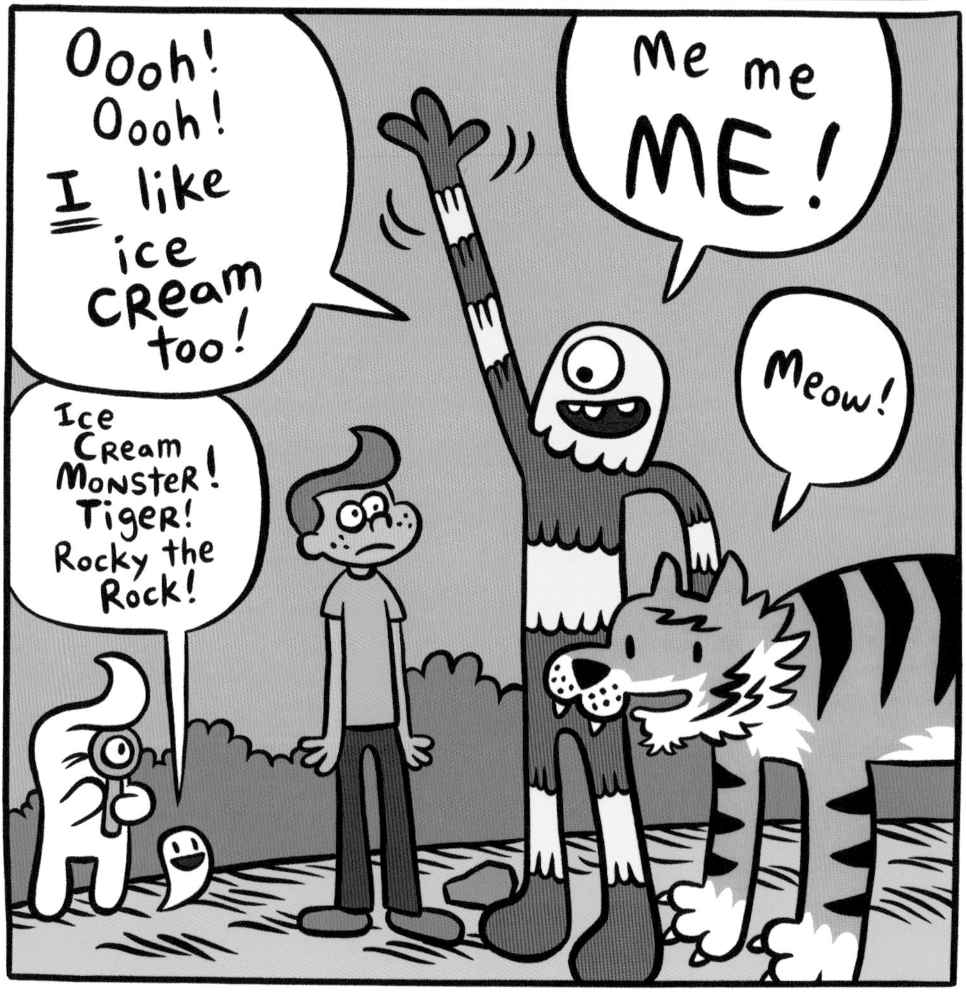
Oooh! Oooh! I like ice cream too!
Me me ME!
Meow!
Ice Cream Monster! Tiger! Rocky the Rock!

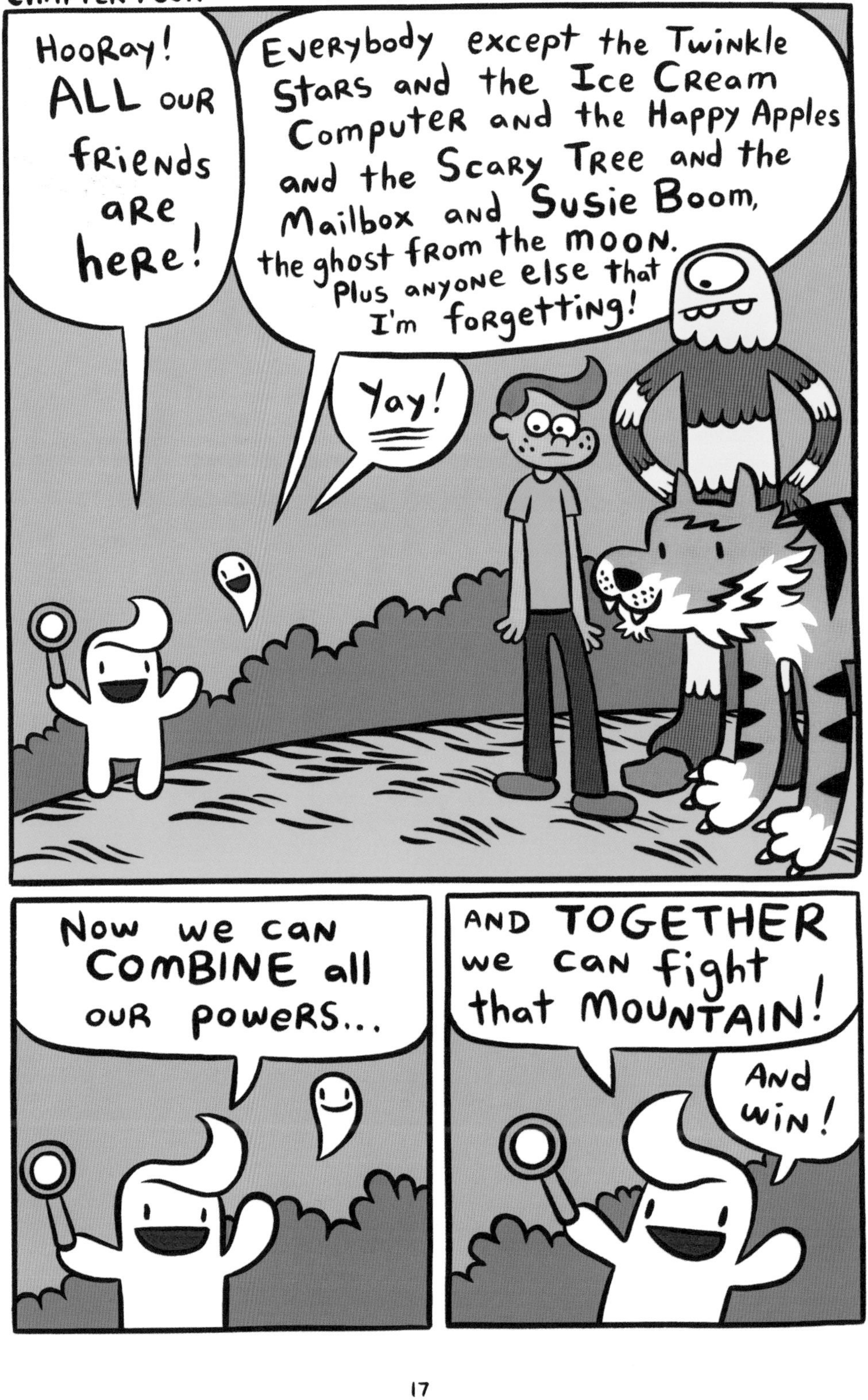
HooRay! ALL our friends are here!
Everybody except the Twinkle Stars and the Ice Cream Computer and the Happy Apples and the Scary Tree and the Mailbox and Susie Boom, the ghost from the moon. Plus anyone else that I'm forgetting!
Yay!
Now we can COMBINE all our powers...
AND TOGETHER we can fight that MOUNTAIN!
And win!

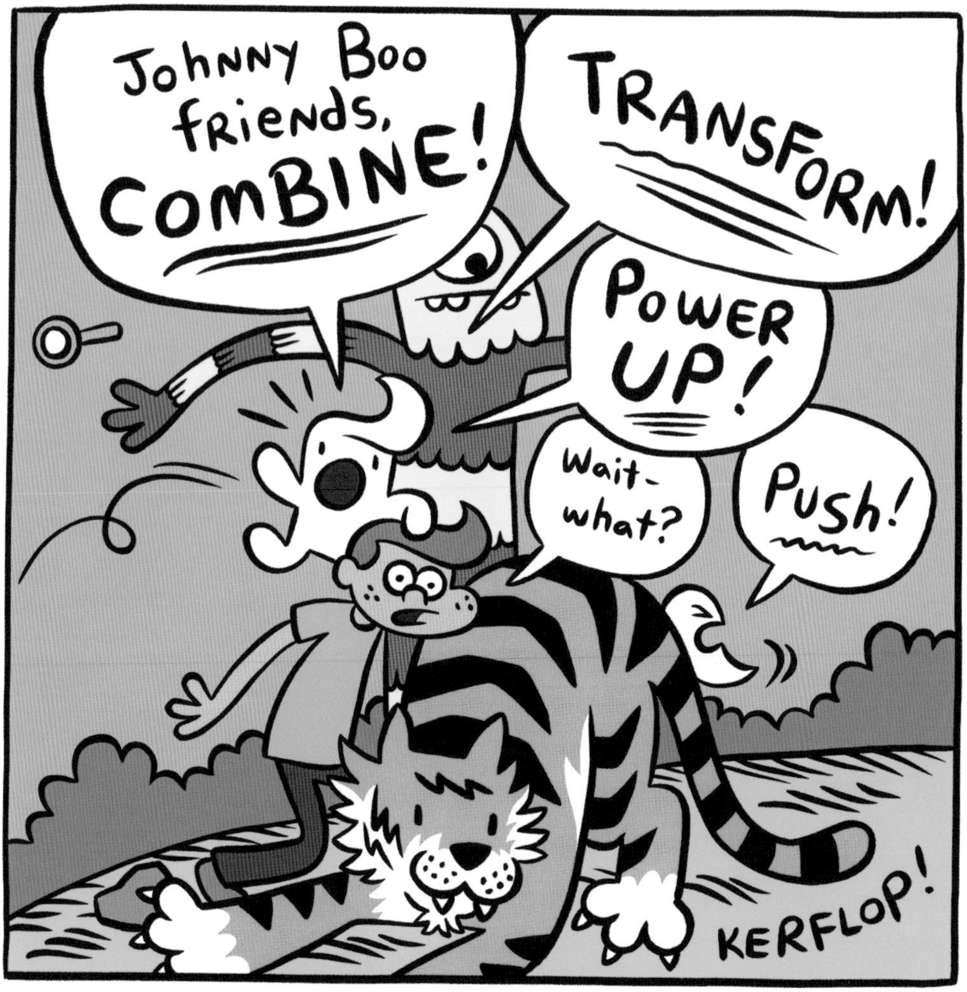
Johnny Boo friends, COMBINE!
TRANSFORM!
POWER UP!
Wait- what?
Push!
KERFLOP!

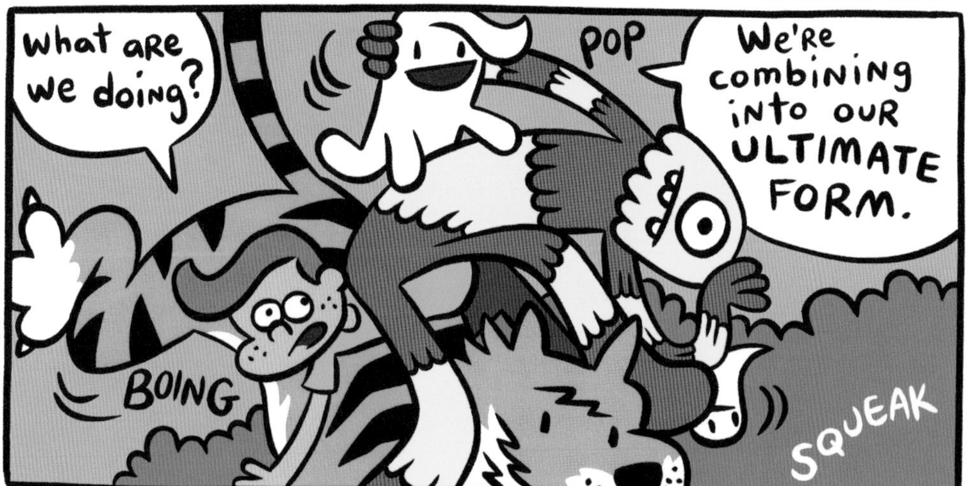
What are we doing?
POP
We're combining into our ULTIMATE FORM.
BOING
SQUEAK

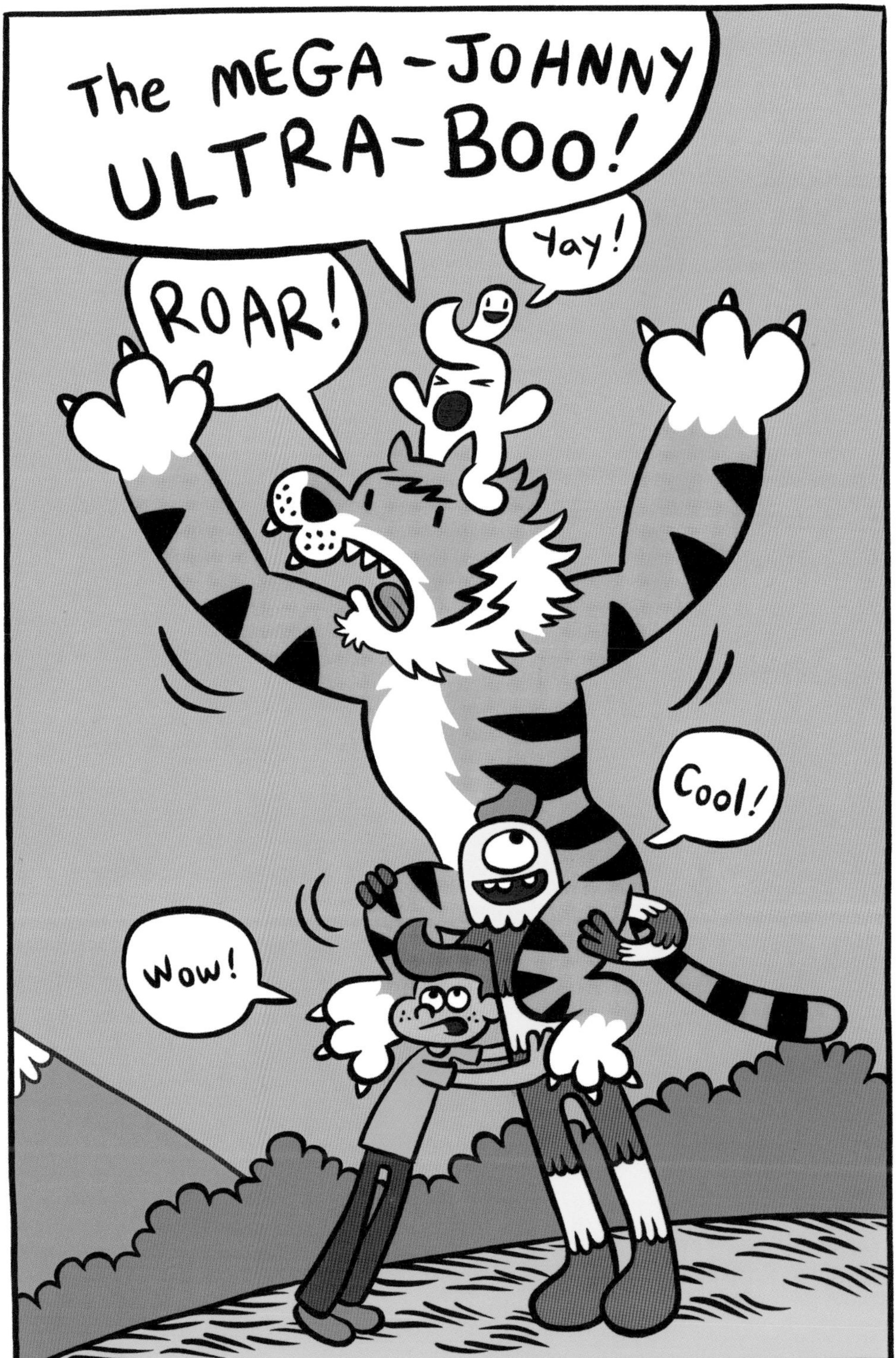
The MEGA-JOHNNY ULTRA-BOO!
ROAR!
Yay!
Cool!
Wow!

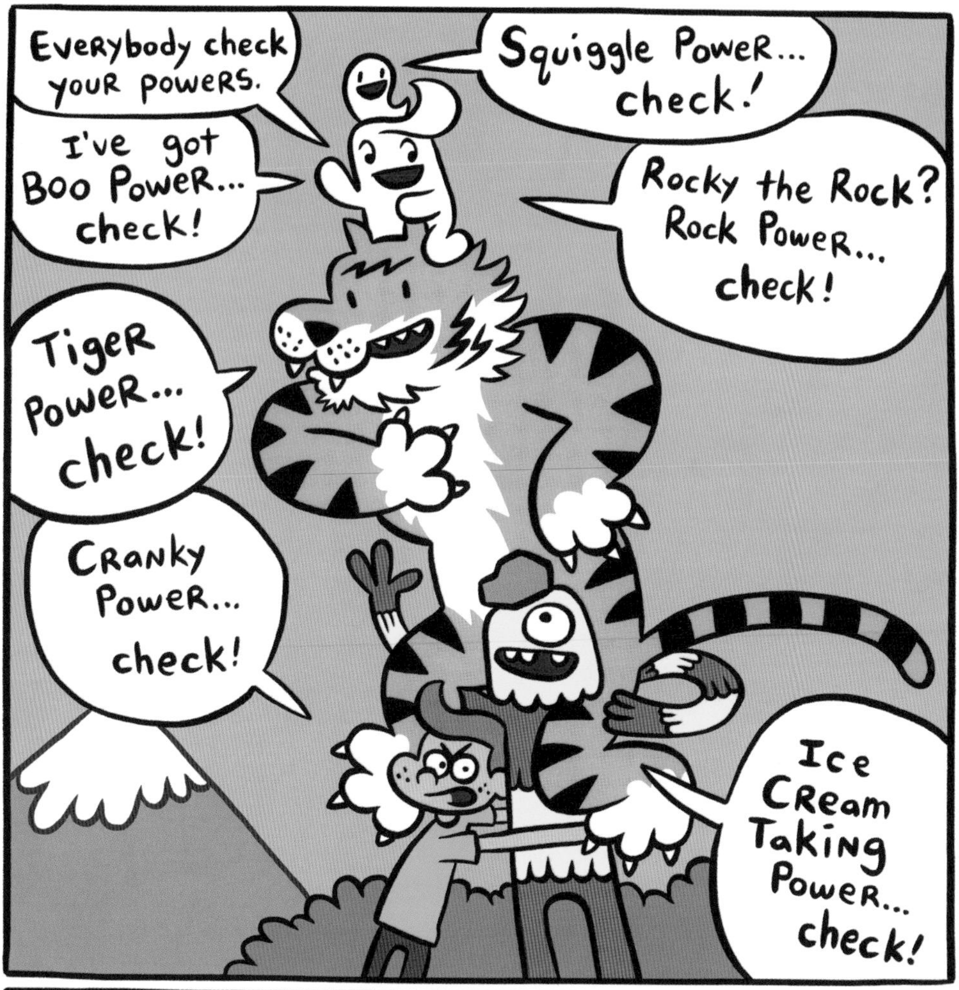
Everybody check your powers.
Squiggle Power... check!
I've got Boo Power... check!
Rocky the Rock? Rock Power... check!
Tiger Power... check!
Cranky Power... check!
Ice Cream Taking Power... check!

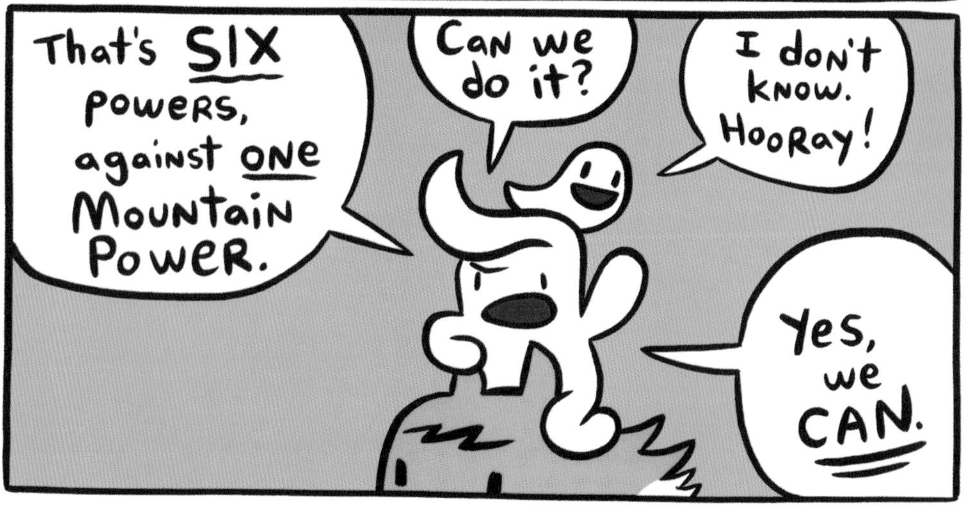
That's SIX powers, against ONE Mountain Power.
Can we do it?
I don't know. Hooray!
Yes, we CAN.

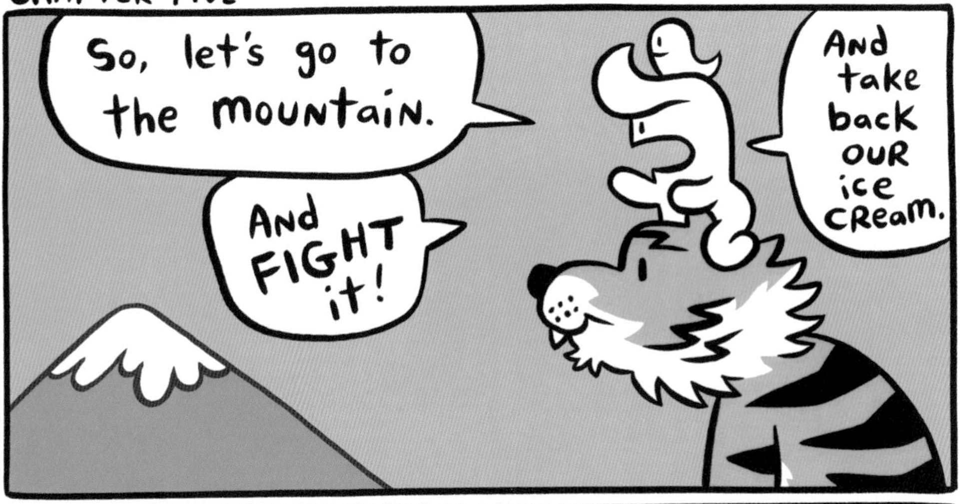
So, let's go to the mountain.
And take back OUR ice cream.
And FIGHT it!

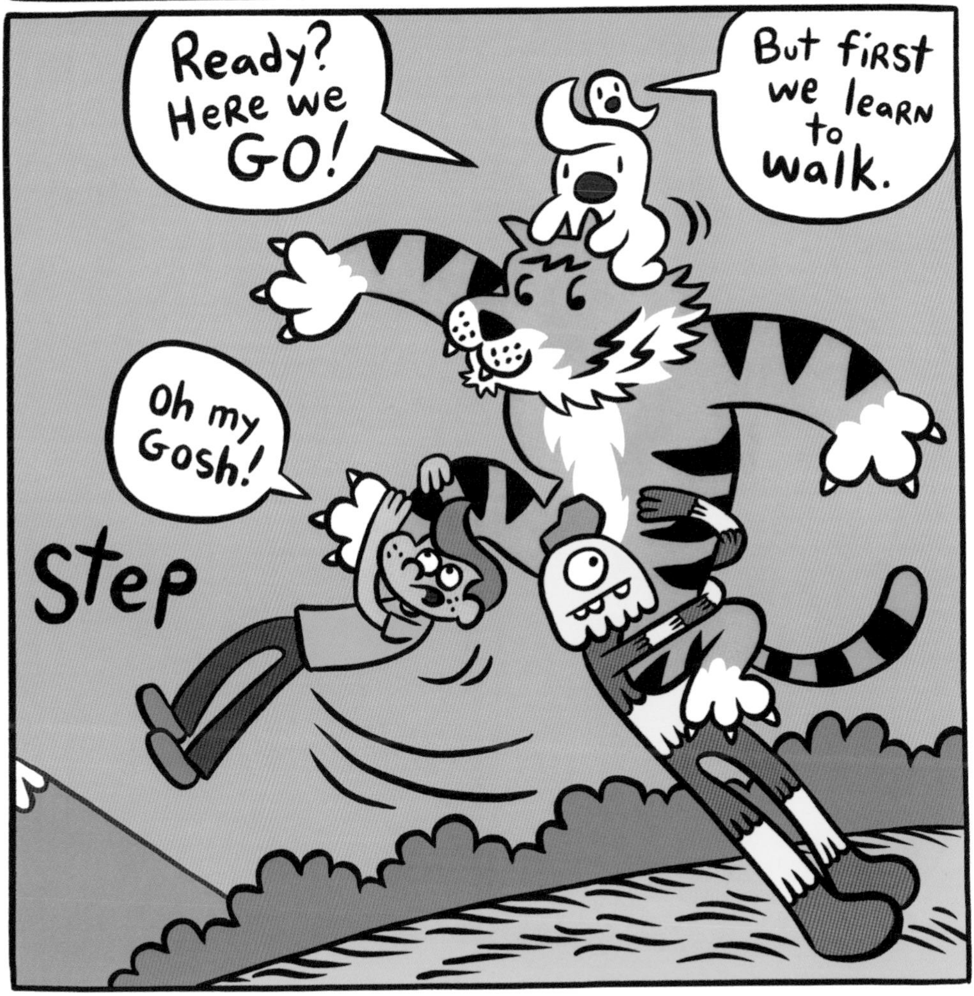
Ready? Here we GO!
But first we learn to walk.
Oh my Gosh!
Step

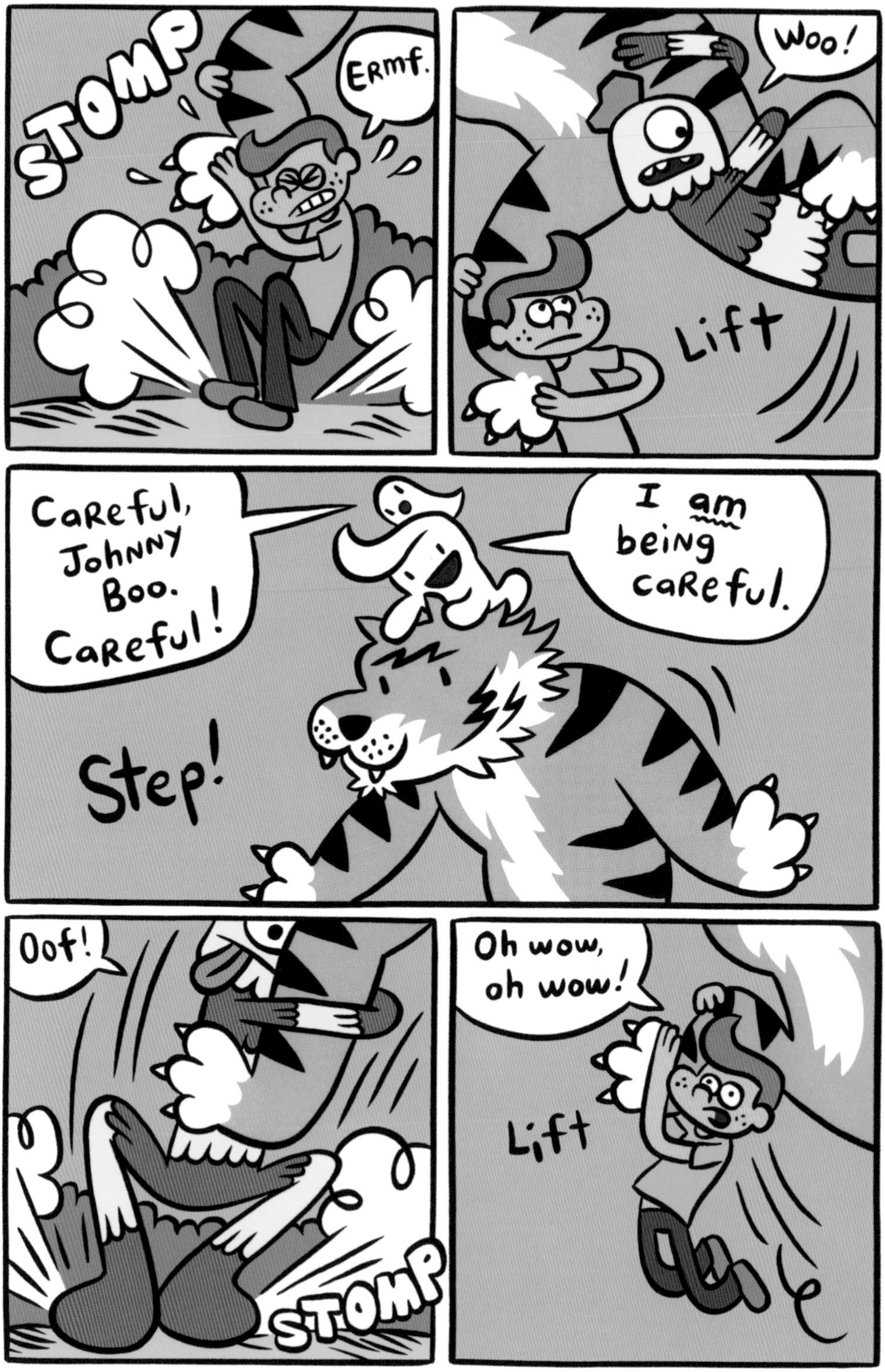
STOMP
ERMF.
Woo!
Lift
Careful, Johnny Boo. Careful!
I am being careful.
Step!
Oof!
STOMP
Oh wow, oh wow!
Lift

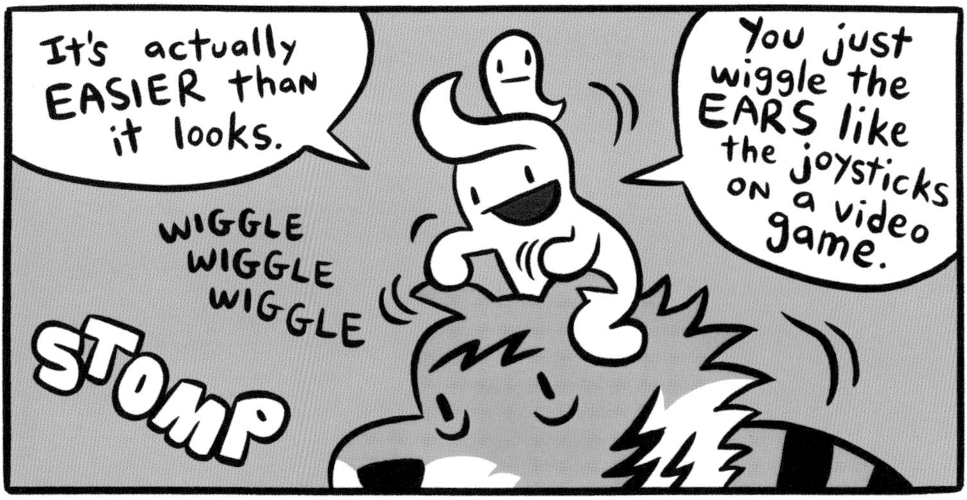
It's actually EASIER than it looks.
You just wiggle the EARS like the joysticks on a video game.
WIGGLE WIGGLE WIGGLE
STOMP

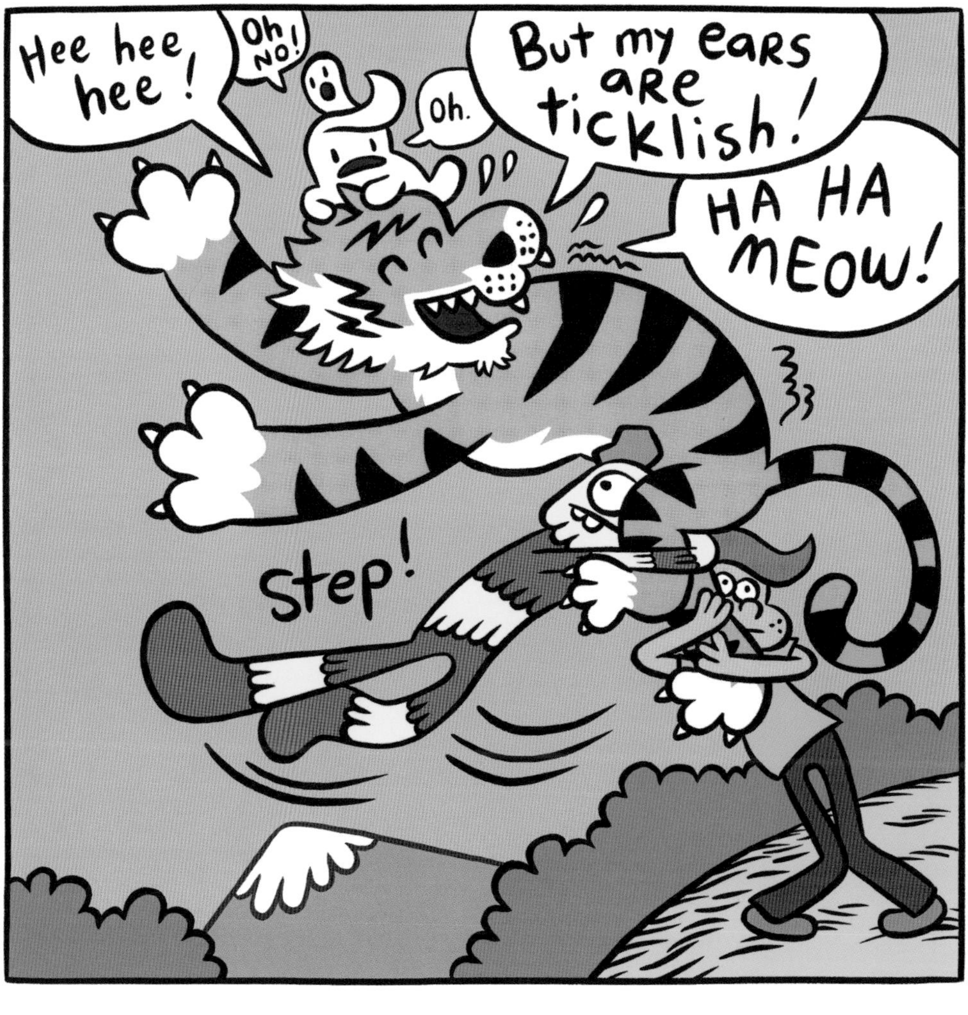
Hee hee hee!
Oh NO!
Oh.
But my ears are ticklish!
HA HA MEOW!
step!

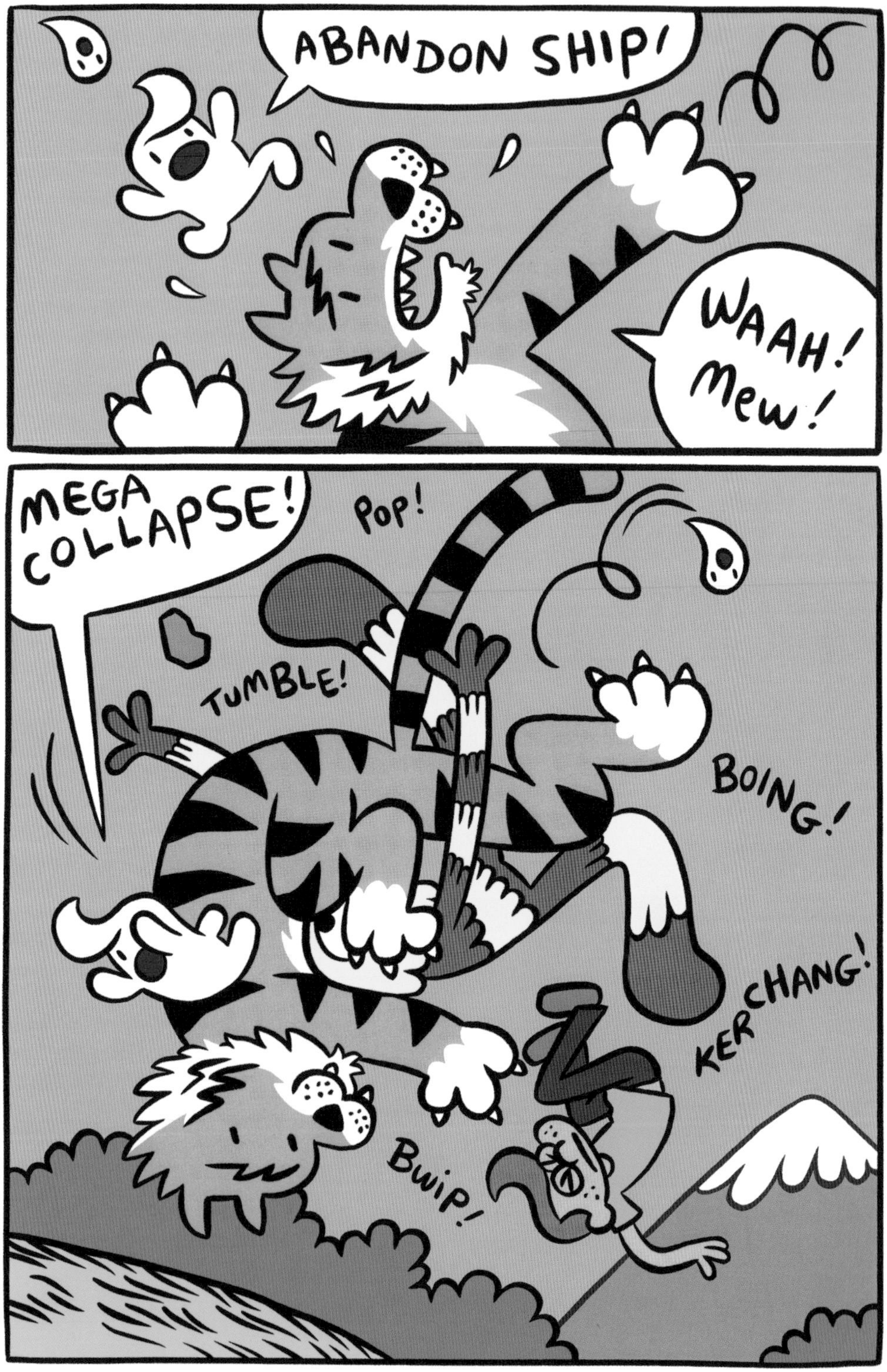
ABANDON SHIP!
WAAH! Mew!
MEGA COLLAPSE!
POP!
TUMBLE!
BOING!
KERCHANG!
BWIP!

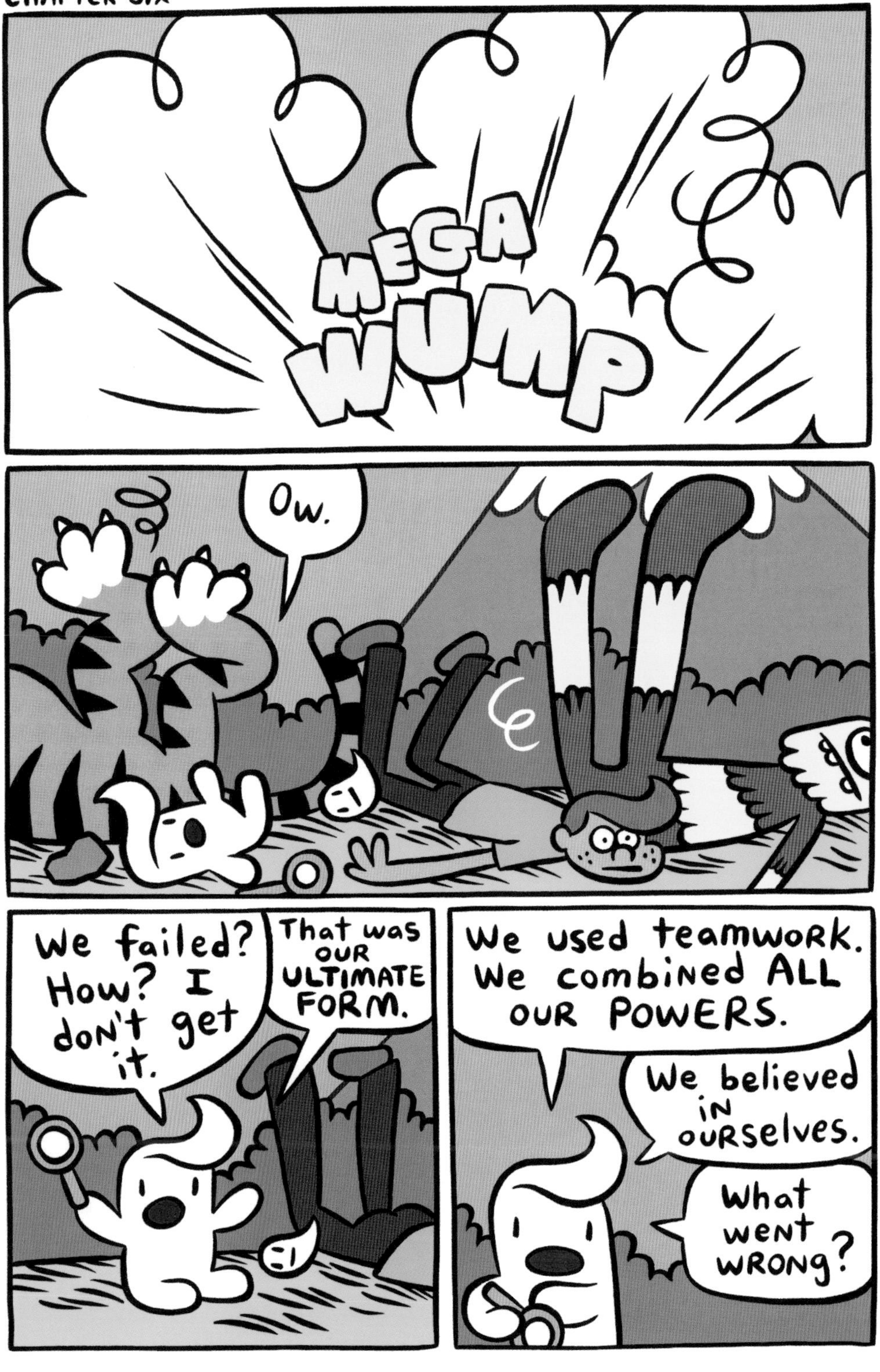
MEGA
WUMP
Ow.
We failed? How? I don't get it.
That was OUR ULTIMATE FORM.
We used teamwork. We combined ALL OUR POWERS.
We believed in ourselves.
What went WRONG?

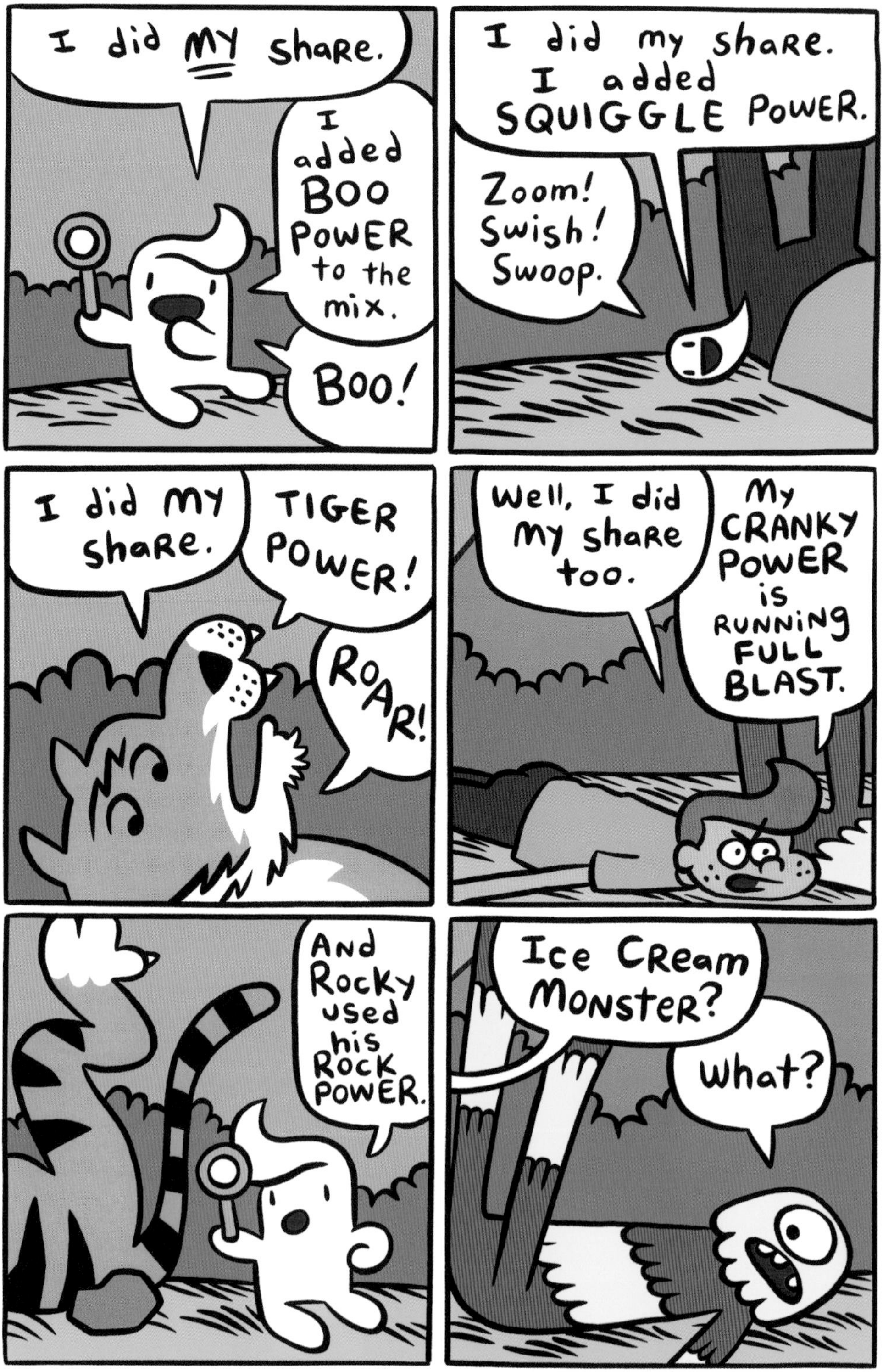

I did MY share.
I added BOO POWER to the mix.
BOO!
I did my share. I added SQUIGGLE POWER.
Zoom! Swish! Swoop.
I did my share.
TIGER POWER!
ROAR!
Well, I did my share too.
My CRANKY POWER is RUNNING FULL BLAST.
AND Rocky used his ROCK POWER.
Ice Cream Monster?
What?

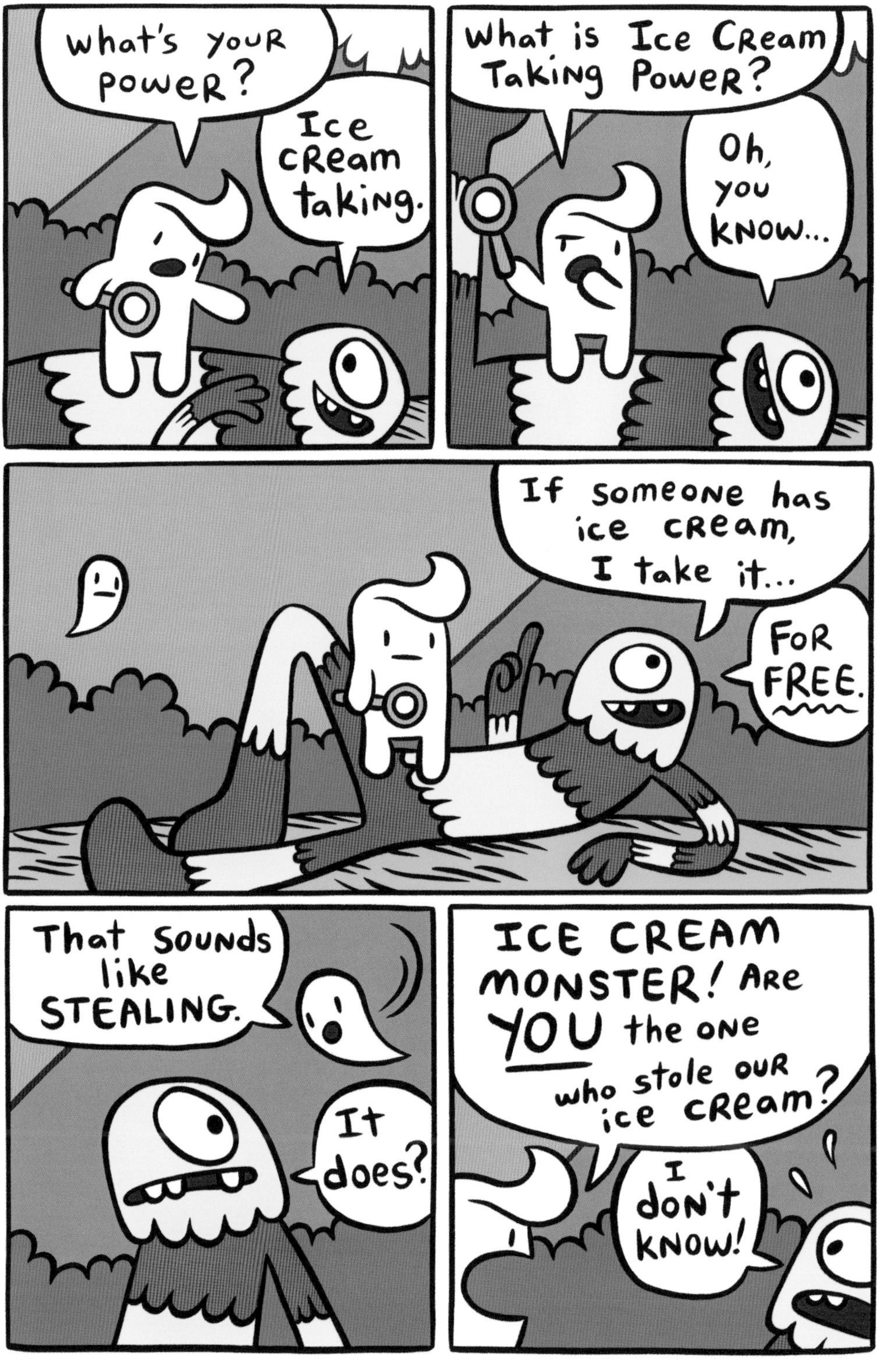
What's your power?
Ice cream taking.
What is Ice Cream Taking Power?
Oh, you know...
If someone has ice cream, I take it...
For FREE.
That sounds like STEALING.
It does?
ICE CREAM MONSTER! Are YOU the one who stole our ice cream?
I don't know!

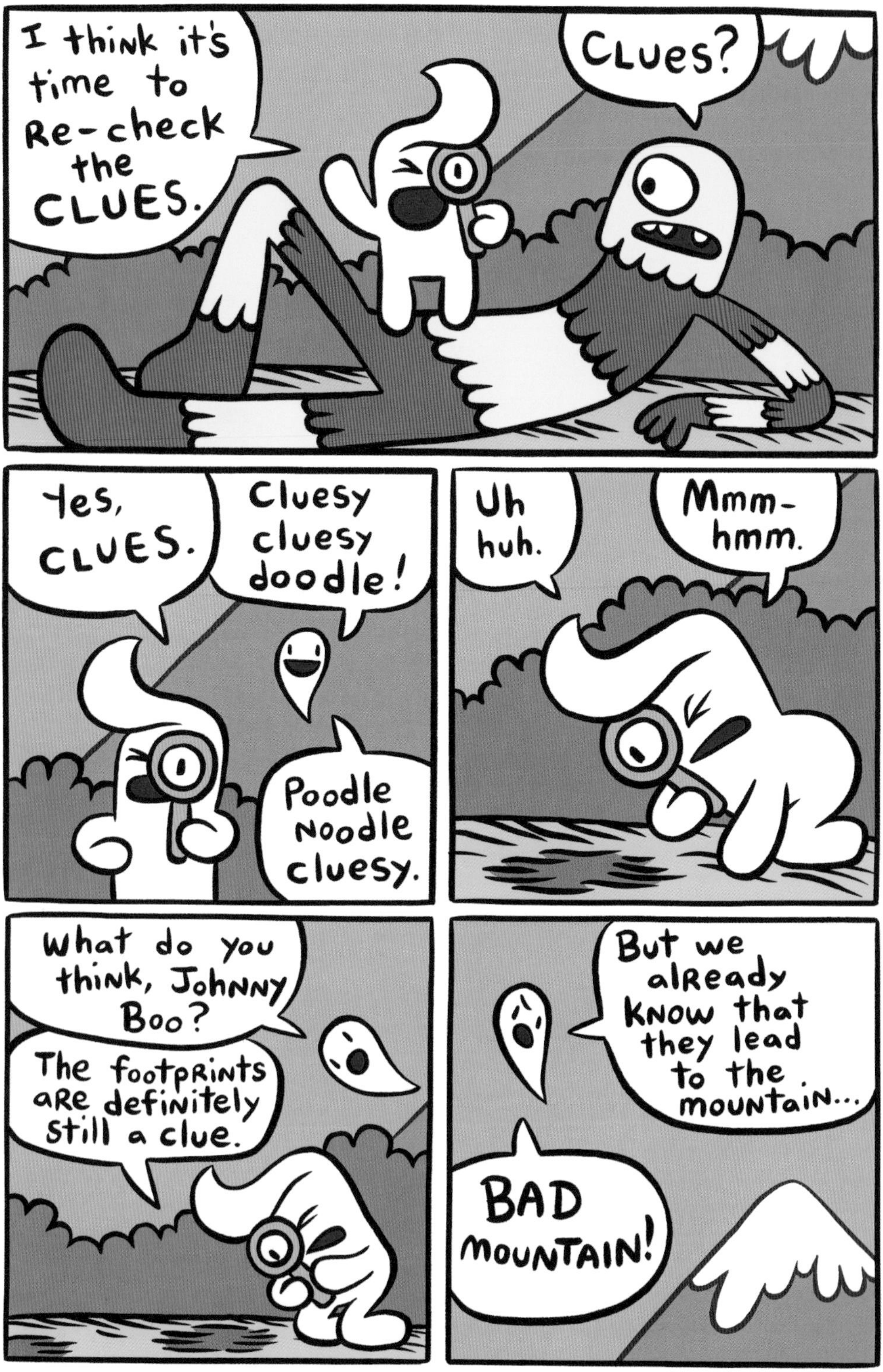
I think it's time to Re-check the CLUES.
CLUES?
Yes, CLUES.
Cluesy cluesy doodle!
Poodle Noodle cluesy.
Uh huh.
Mmm-hmm.
What do you think, Johnny Boo?
The footprints are definitely still a clue.
But we already know that they lead to the mountain...
BAD MOUNTAIN!

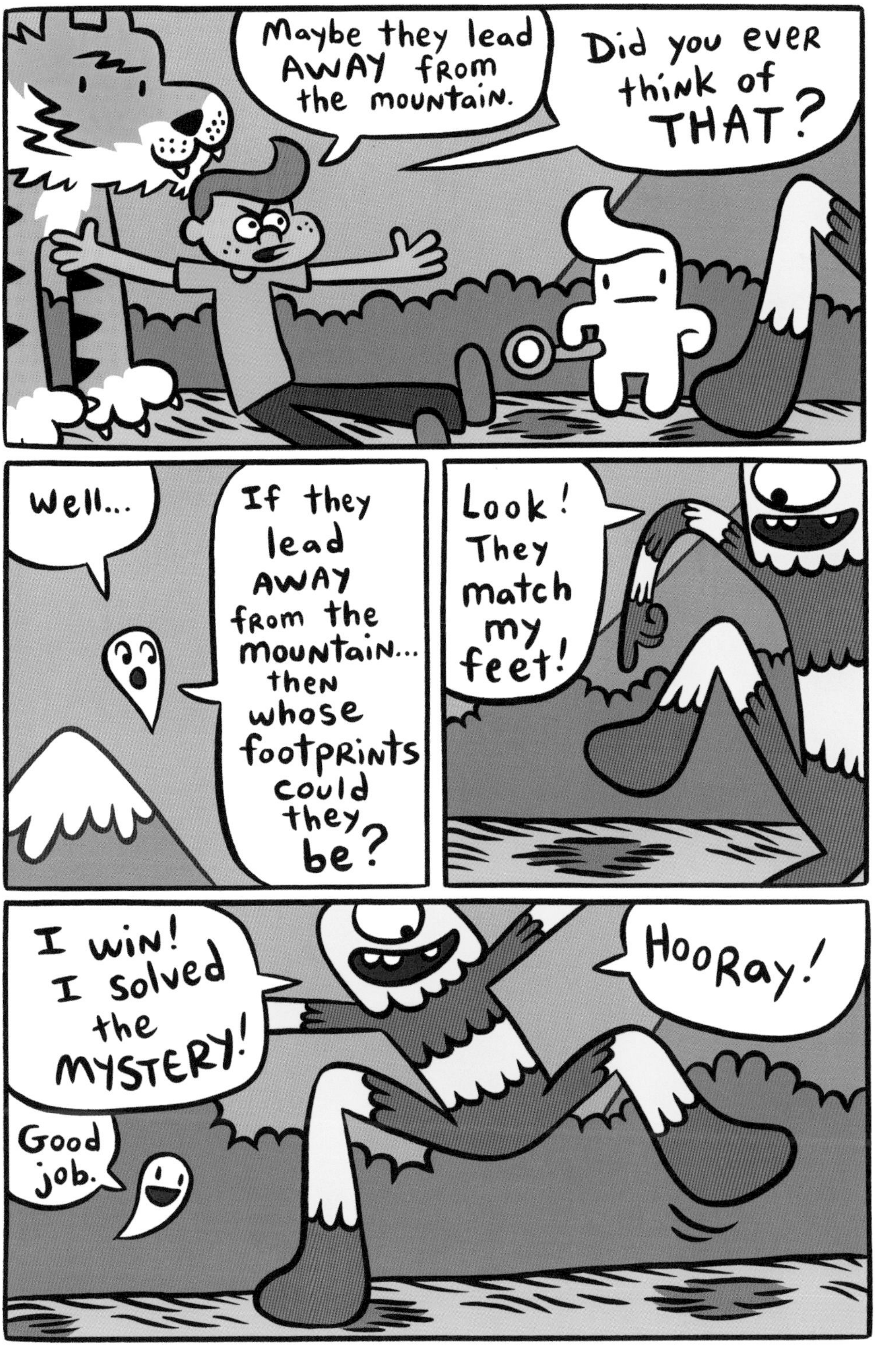
Maybe they lead AWAY FROM the mountain.
Did you ever think of THAT?
Well...
If they lead AWAY from the mountain... then whose footprints could they be?
Look! They match my feet!
I win! I solved the MYSTERY!
HooRay!
Good job.

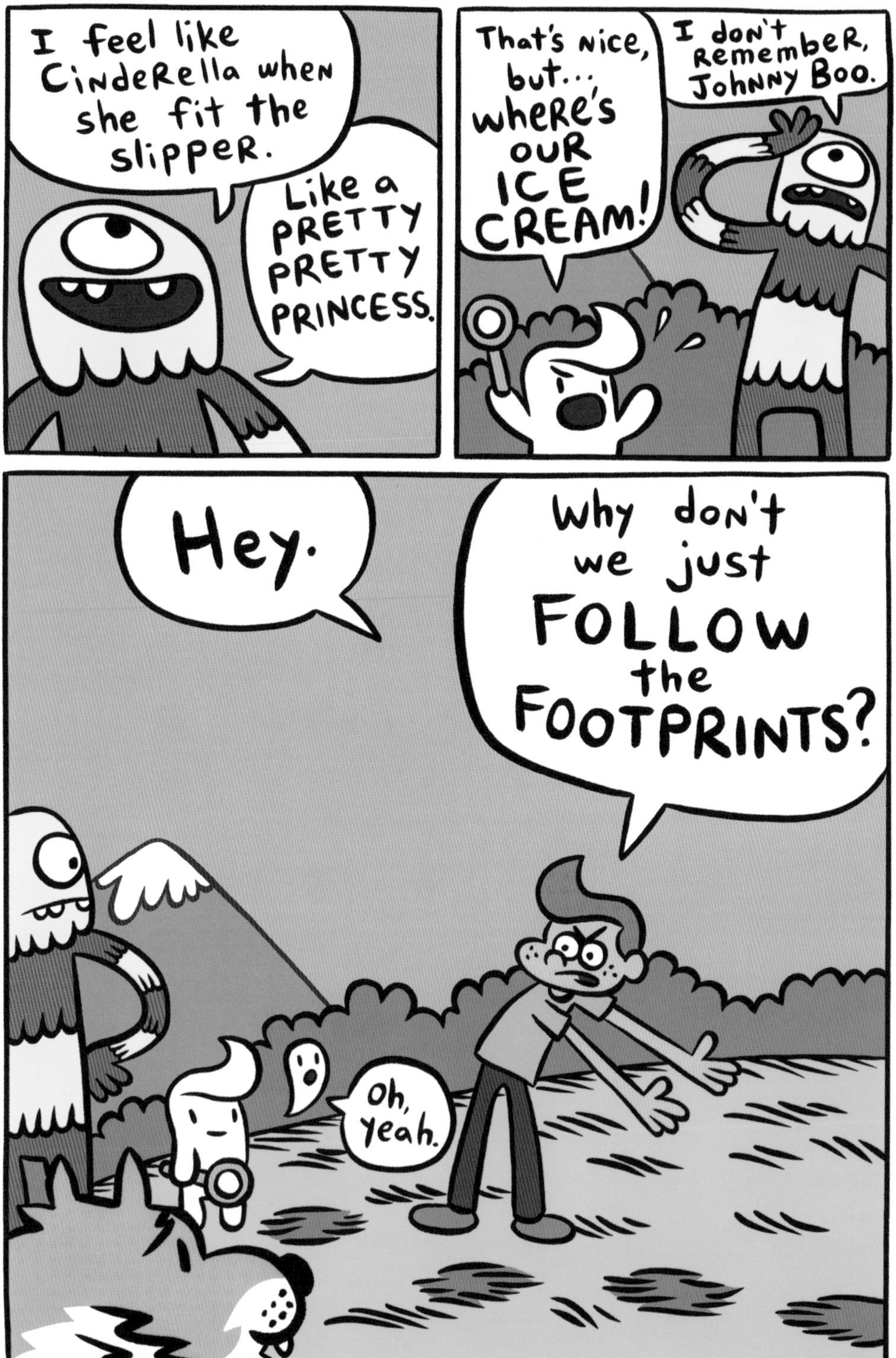
I feel like Cinderella when she fit the slipper.
Like a PRETTY PRETTY PRINCESS.
That's nice, but... where's OUR ICE CREAM!
I don't remember, Johnny Boo.
Hey.
Why don't we just FOLLOW the FOOTPRINTS?
Oh, yeah.

CHAPTER SEVEN

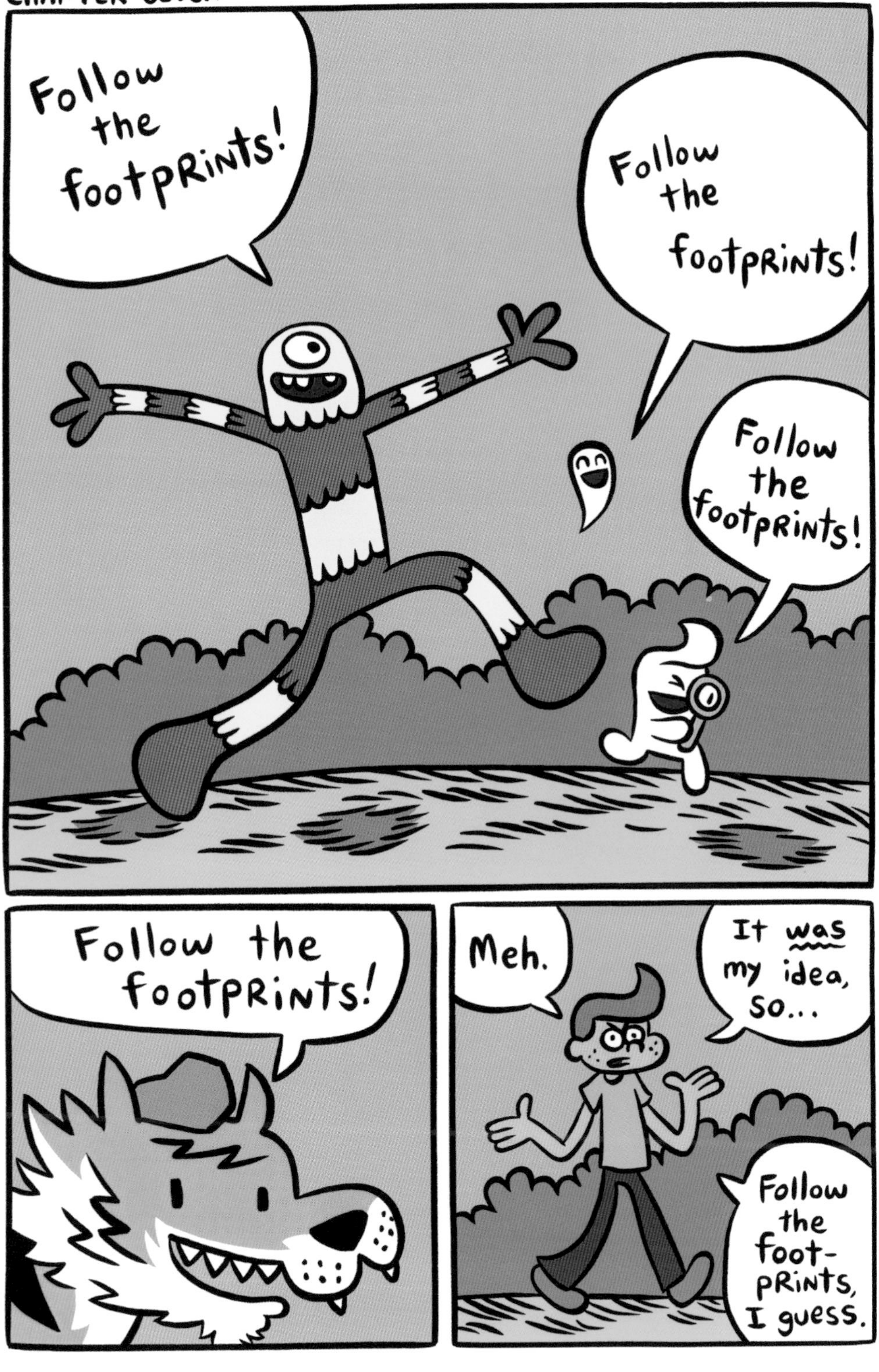
Follow the footprints!
Follow the footprints!
Follow the footprints!
Follow the footprints!
Meh.
It was my idea, so...
Follow the foot-prints, I guess.

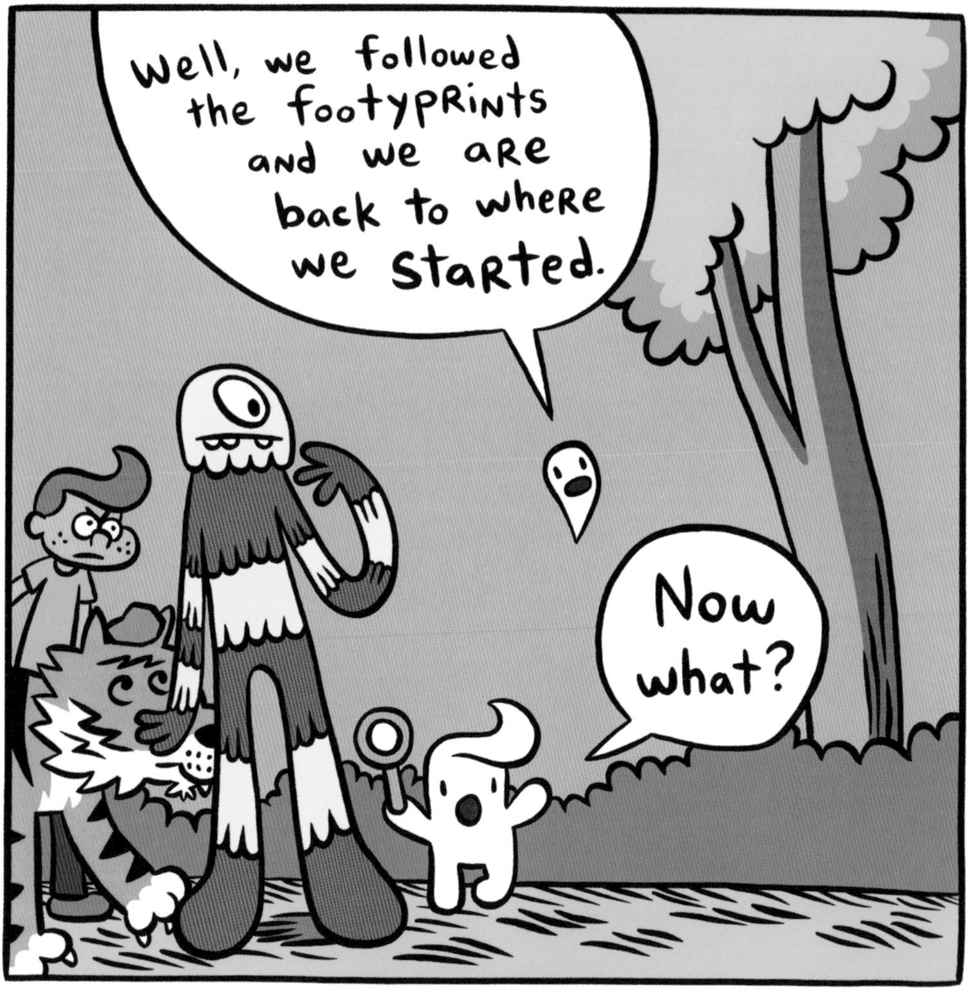
Well, we followed the footyprints and we are back to where we started.
Now what?

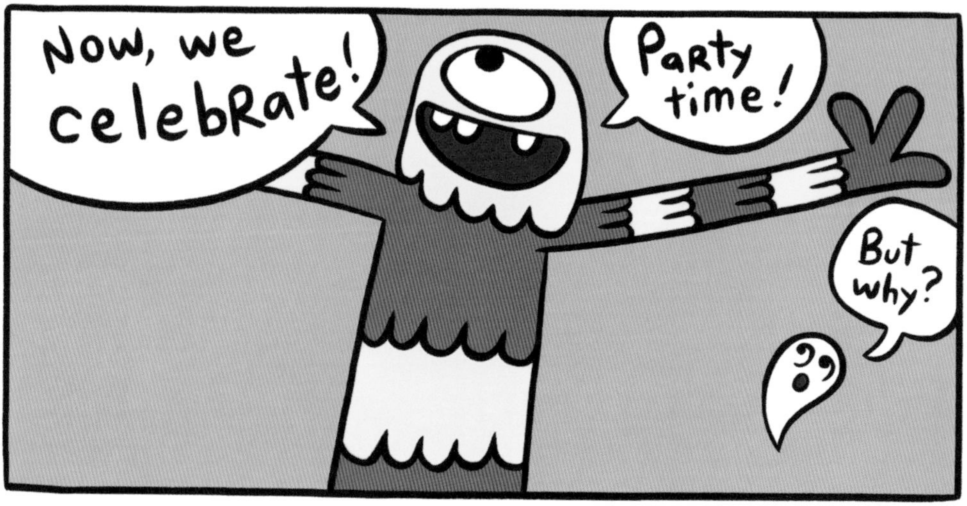
Now, we celebrate!
Party time!
But why?

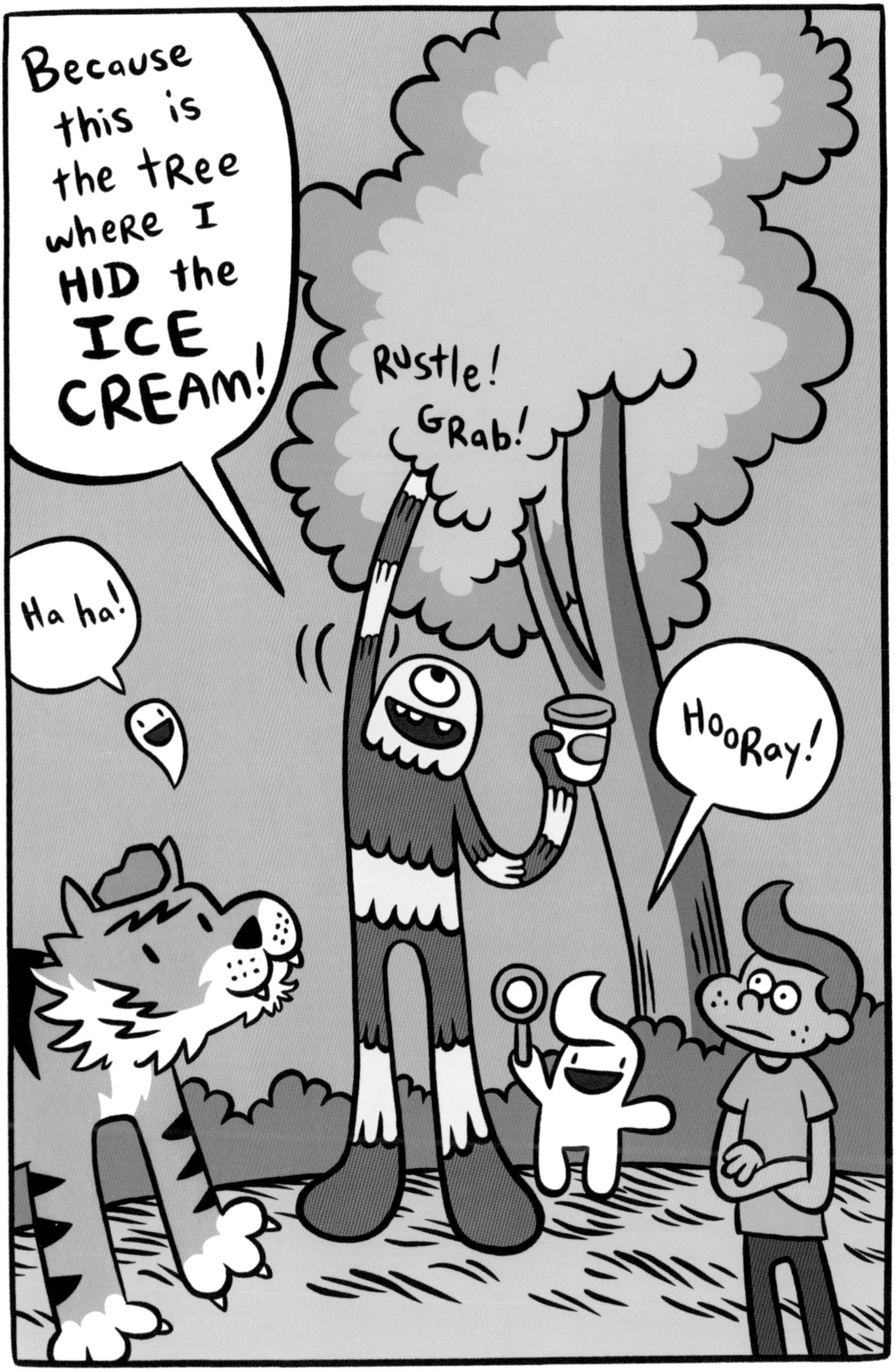
Because this is the tree where I HID the ICE CREAM!
Rustle!
Grab!
Ha ha!
HooRay!

CHAPTER EIGHT

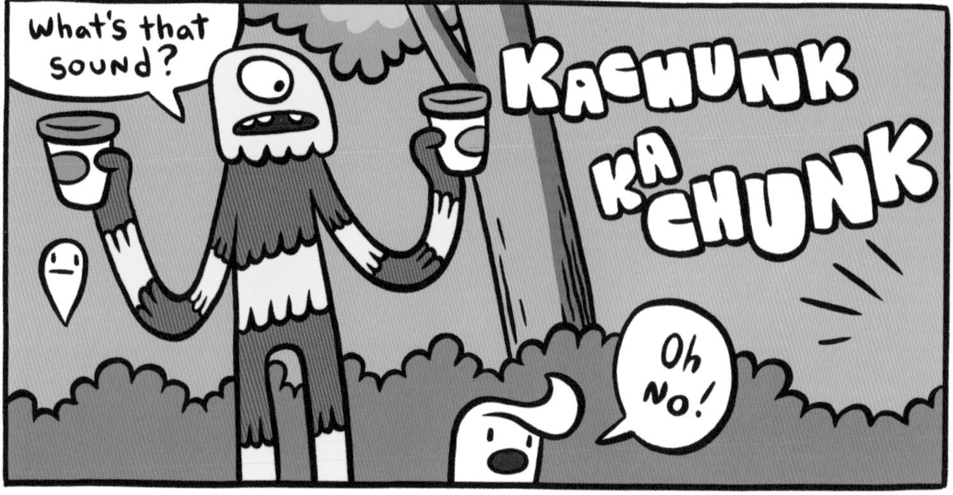

What's that sound?
KACHUNK
KA CHUNK
Oh No!

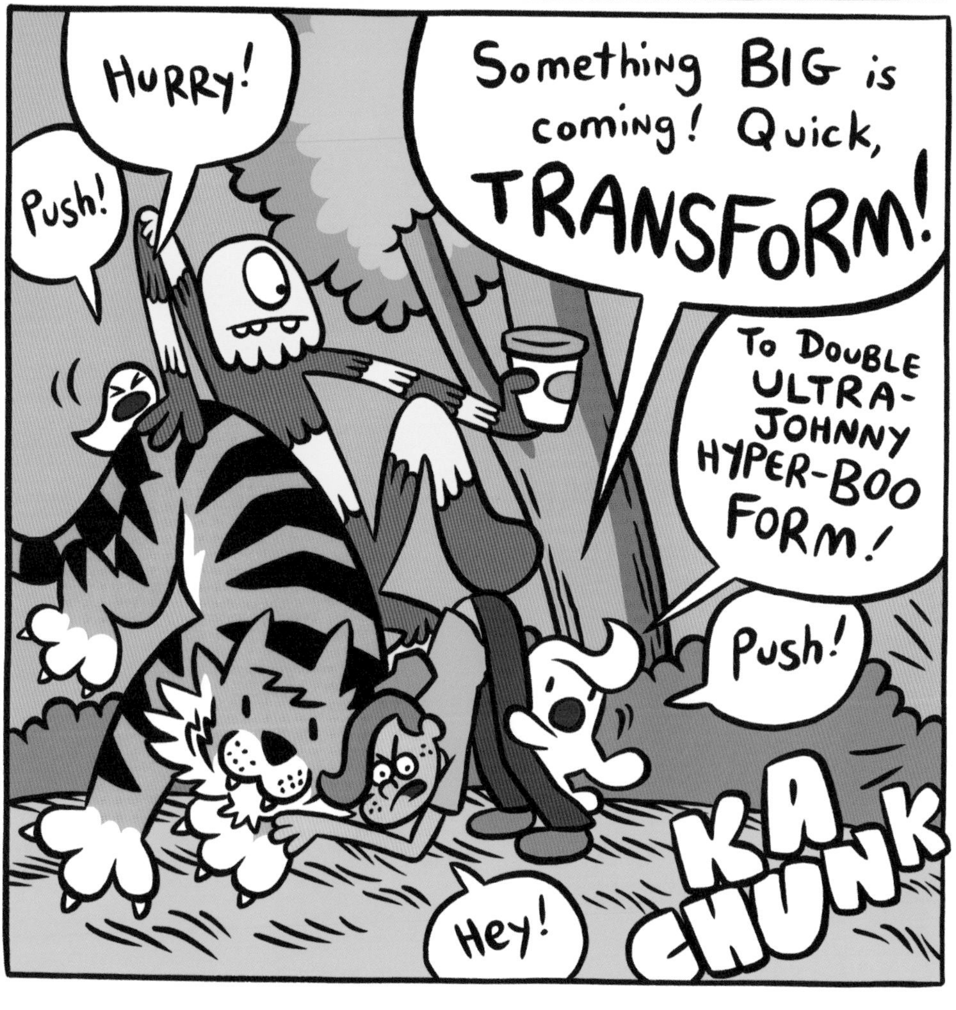

HURRY!
Push!
Something BIG is coming! Quick, TRANSFORM!
To DOUBLE ULTRA-JOHNNY HYPER-BOO FORM!
Push!
KA CHUNK
Hey!

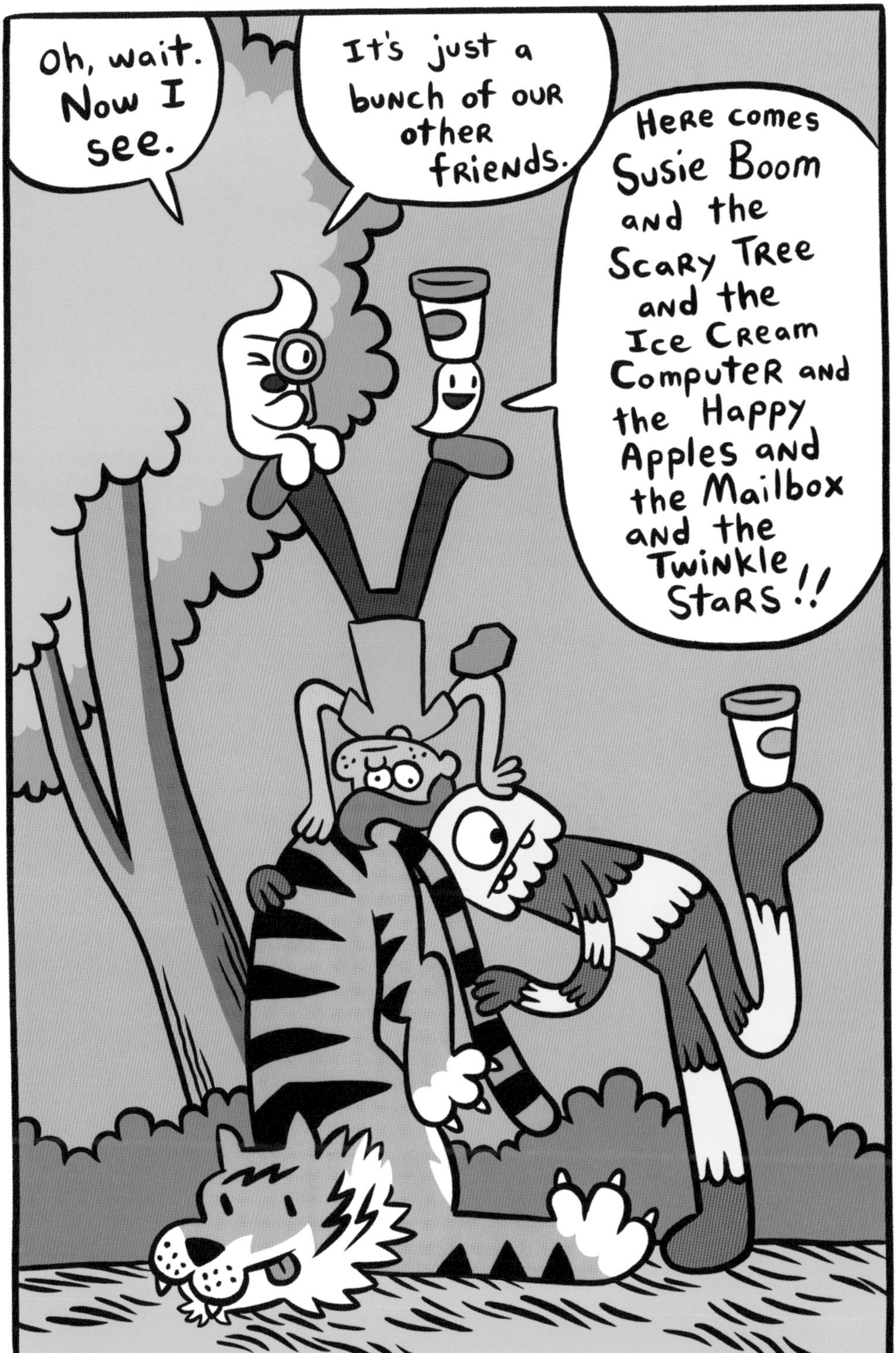
Oh, wait. Now I see.
It's just a bunch of our other friends.
Here comes Susie Boom and the Scary Tree and the Ice Cream Computer and the Happy Apples and the Mailbox and the Twinkle Stars!!

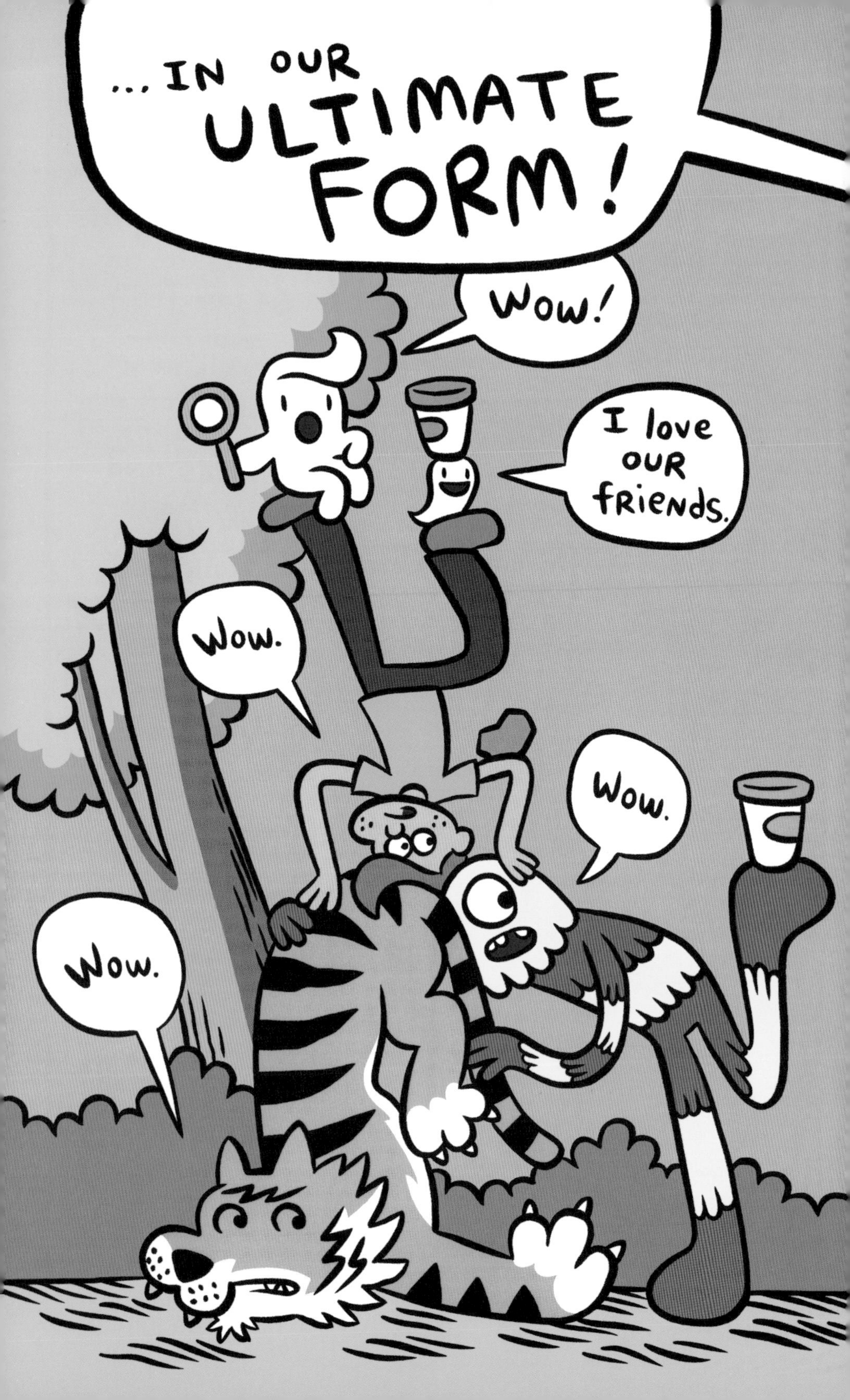

...IN OUR ULTIMATE FORM!
Wow!
I love our friends.
Wow.
Wow.
Wow.

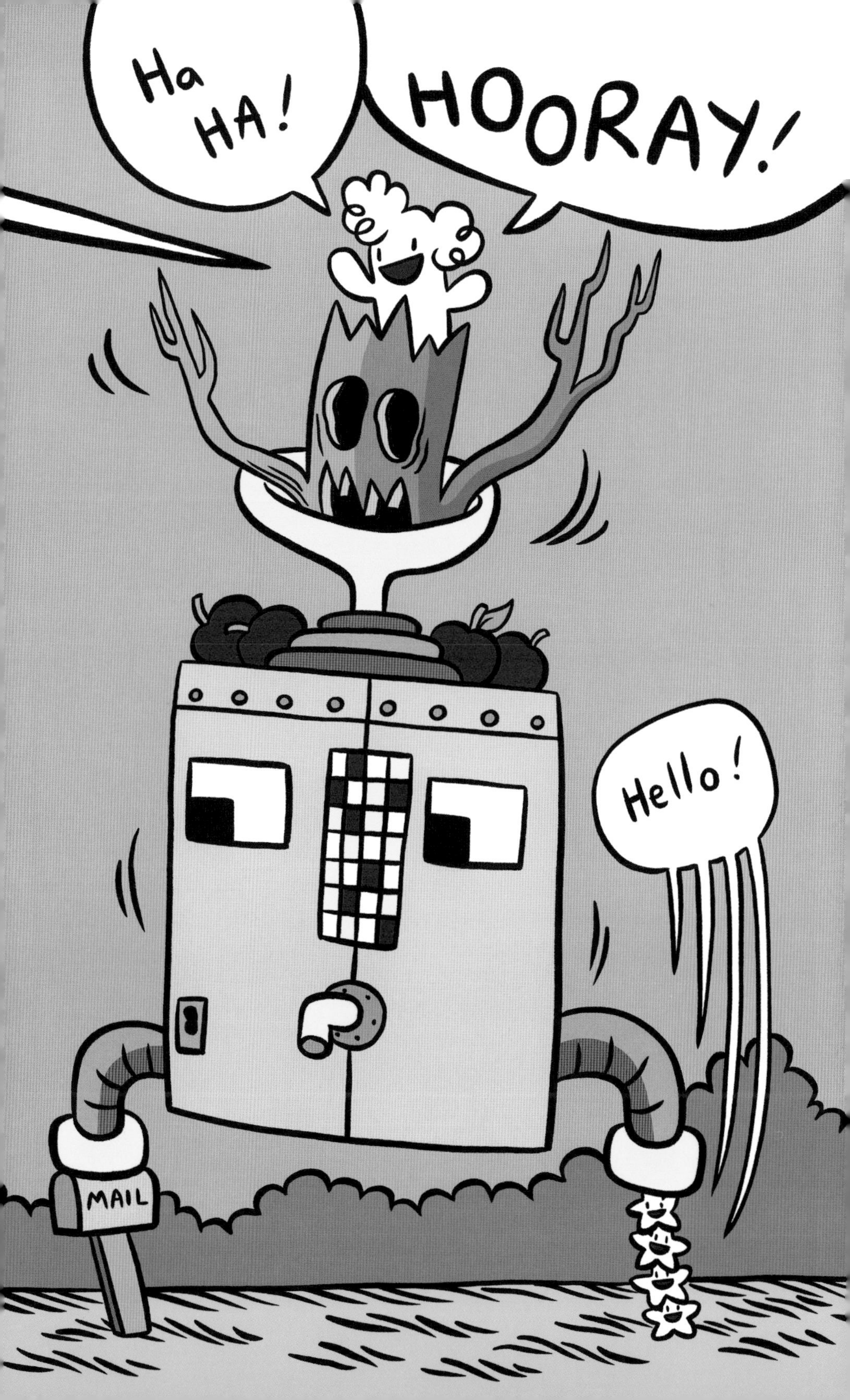
Ha HA!
HOORAY!
Hello!
MAIL

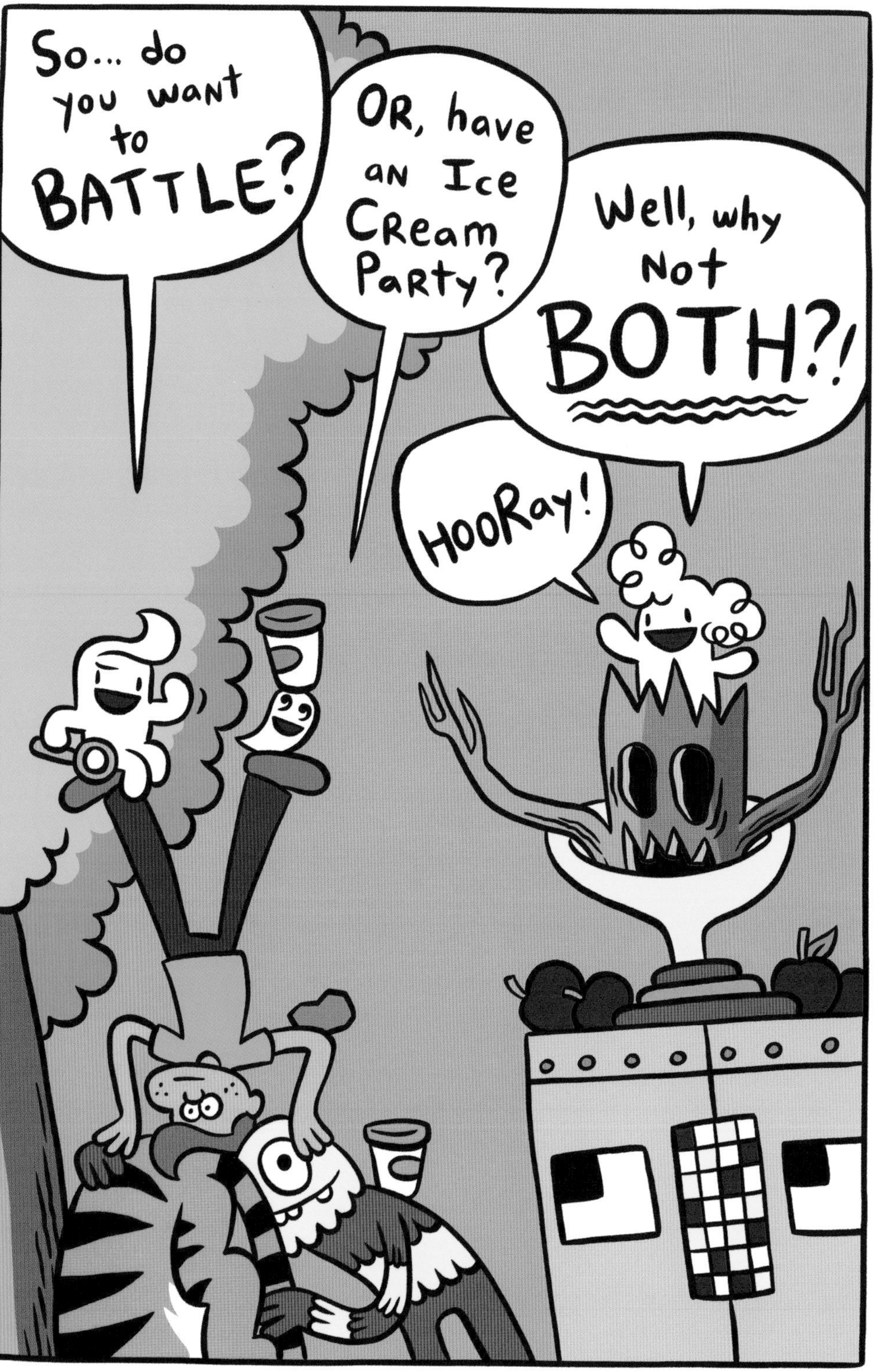
So... do you want to BATTLE?
OR, have an Ice Cream Party?
Well, why Not BOTH?!
HOORay!

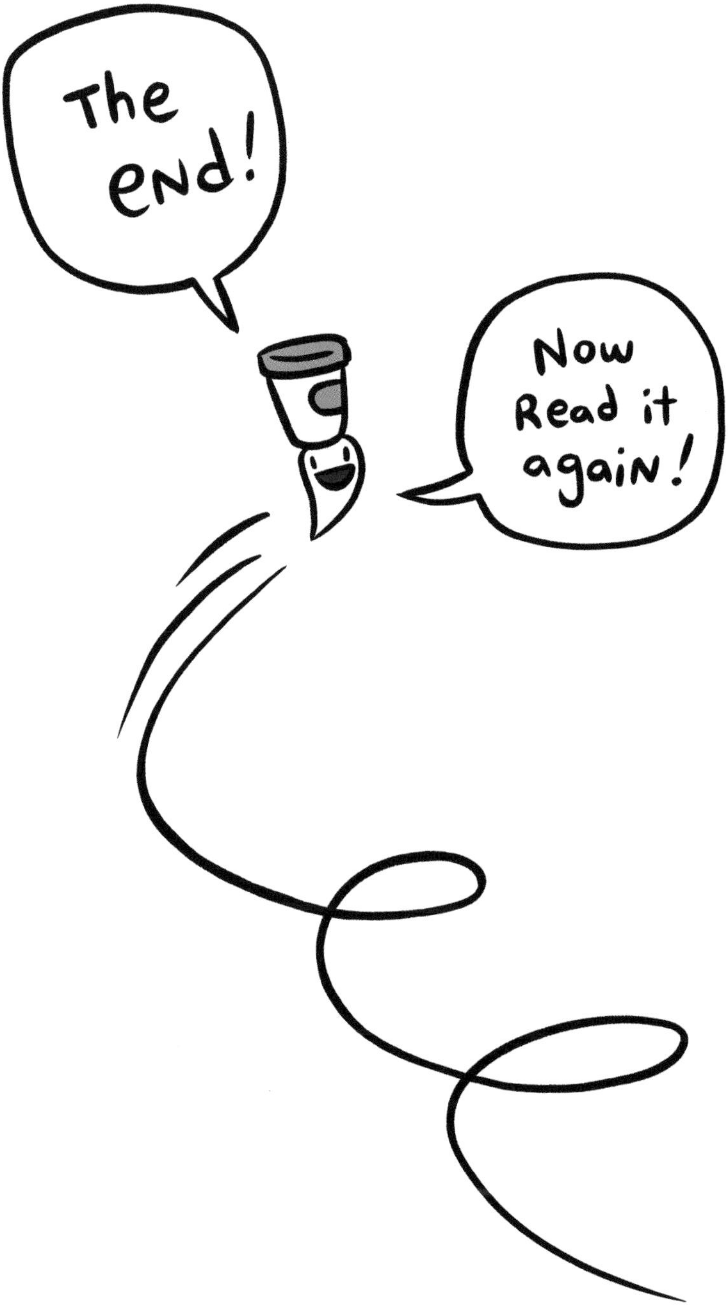
The end!
Now Read it again!

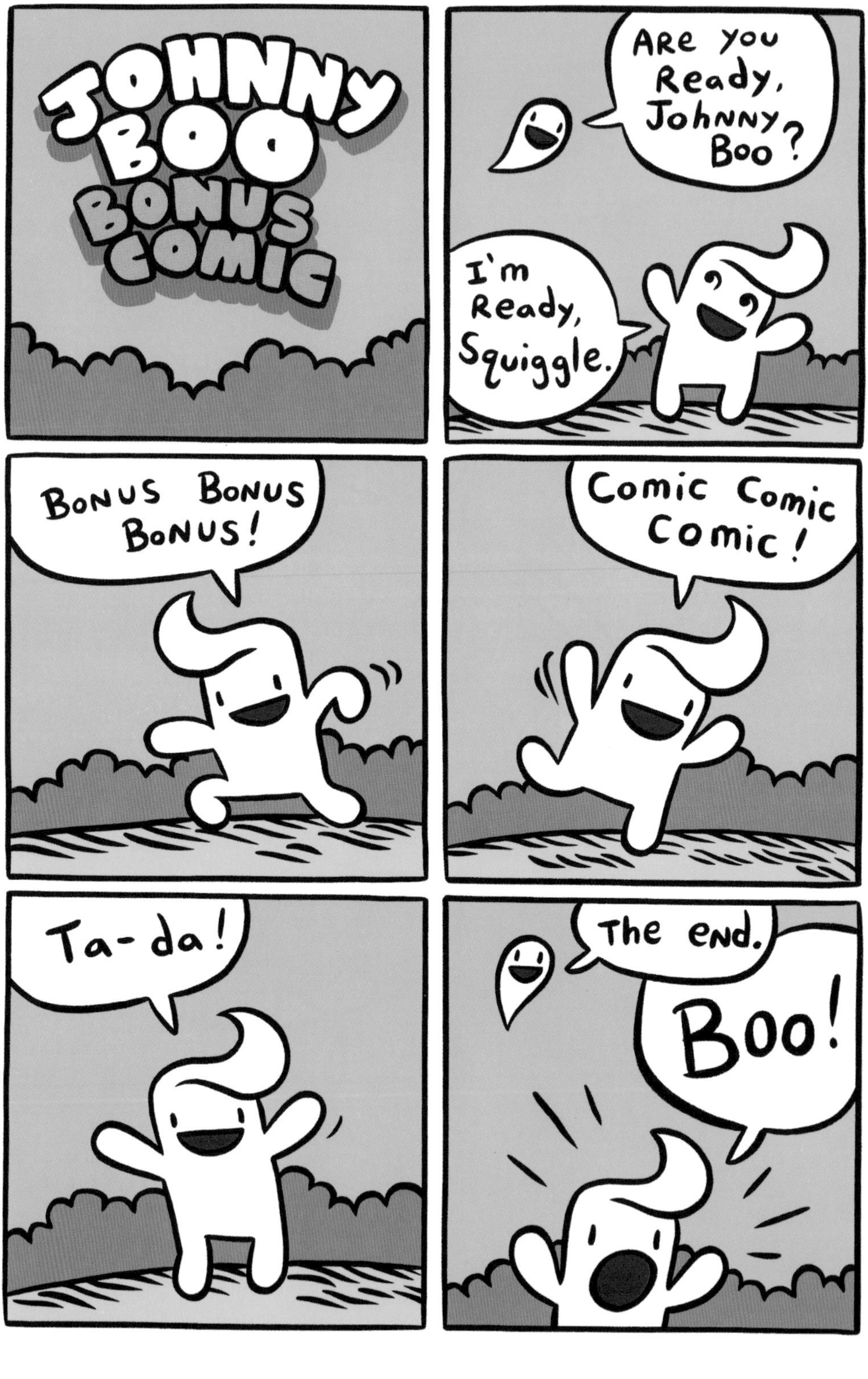
JOHNNY BOO BONUS COMIC
Are you Ready, Johnny Boo?
I'm Ready, Squiggle.
BONUS BONUS BONUS!
Comic Comic Comic!
Ta-da!
The end.
Boo!